Sherlock Holmes and The Railway Maniac

'Nothing would tempt me back to my old career on any but the most temporary basis.' This categoric statement was made by the great consulting detective, Sherlock Holmes, now into his third year of retirement, to his old partner and friend, Dr John H. Watson, MD. But his resolve was to be short lived.

At the behest of his enigmatic brother, Mycroft, Holmes is persuaded to investigate two unexplained, catastrophic train derailments which have caused the deaths of more than forty people. Why would a criminal wreck an express train?

A strange astronomer, the German Intelligence Service, a Russian yacht in the port of Aberdeen – the clues accumulate while the most homicidal lunatic in Britain remains at large. Something was afoot in Scotland that drew both King Edward VII and Mycroft Holmes from their lairs in Sandringham and Whitehall. A meeting with an emissary of the Czar?

The strenuous efforts of Sherlock Holmes to avert an international calamity and to bring to justice an evil assassin are here revealed for the first time in a tale the late Sir Arthur himself would have been proud of.

SHERLOCK HOLMES
AND THE
RAILWAY MANIAC

A Narrative believed to be from the pen of
John H. Watson, MD

Annotated and Edited for publication by
Barrie Roberts

This edition published in Great Britain in 2001 by
Allison & Busby Limited
Suite 111, Bon Marche Centre
241-251 Ferndale Road
London SW9 8BJ
http://www.allisonandbusby.ltd.uk

First published by Constable & Company Ltd

The right of Barrie Roberts to be identified as
author of this work has been asserted by him in
accordance with the Copyright, Designs and
Patents Act, 1988

A catalogue record for this book is available from
the British Library.

ISBN 0 7490 0546 7

Printed and bound in Spain by
Liberduplex, s.l. Barcelona.

CONTENTS

INTRODUCTION

The accompanying text is an edited version of a document which came into my hands some years ago. To all appearances it is one of the lost or suppressed 'records' of John H. Watson, the companion and chronicler of the cases of Sherlock Holmes.

Of its origins I can discover nothing, save that it seems to have been for a long time in the possession of an ancestor of mine who was both a medical man and a contemporary of Watson.

Before putting it before the public I have made such checks as were possible. Those who claim familiarity with Watson's handwriting (though no unassailable specimen is known to exist) agree that the manuscript appears to be in his hand, and the narrative displays the usual Watsonian mixture of real and invented personal and place-names.

There are several political and historical details mentioned in the manuscript which appear to confirm its authenticity, and these are discussed in detailed notes at the end. Some would bear more attention than I have been able to give them, and it may well be that greater expertise than mine could prove the document's origin beyond a doubt.

In the mean time I can only assert that I am as satisfied as I can be that this narrative is the work of Dr Watson and that, in arranging for it to be published, I am making public an authentic account of the last case of the world's first consulting detective, Sherlock Holmes.

Barrie Roberts
Walsall, September 1993

1

AN INTERRUPTED HOLIDAY

After so many years of recording the exploits of my friend Sherlock Holmes, it seems strange to begin this new chronicle in the knowledge that it is unlikely to be read by the public for a good many years, if at all.

In the more than thirty years of my association with Holmes there were always, of course, cases whose details I could not lay before the public. Some were matters involving persons so distinctive that no pseudonym could disguise their identities, while others involved subjects too repellent for general publication. A third group, often involving Holmes' brother Mycroft, bore upon matters of national interest, where simple patriotism forbade any revelations that might aid a potential enemy or reveal too much of the inward workings of government.

The case which I now set down falls, partly, into all of those categories, inasmuch as it concerned a member of our Royal Family, it involved the most vital and delicate international negotiations, and it embodied a series of crimes, so fiendish in their conception and execution, and so widespread in their effects that, had they been revealed at the time, the revulsion and anger of the public would have passed all imagining and might well have plunged our country into war. If I now commit the details to paper, it is not to satisfy any idle or sensationalist reader, but rather to leave as true and complete a record as I may of the strenuous efforts of Sherlock Holmes to avert an international calamity and to bring to justice the most evil assassin that this country has ever known. Posterity should know of the singular exertions of my friend in a matter where it is no exaggeration to say that the peace of Europe hung in the balance.

The affair first came into Holmes' hands in the autumn of 1906, when he had been nearly three years retired. During those years there had been no shortage of pleas for his assistance, some of which had come from those well able to reward his efforts, but most of them he turned away, continuing to find his intellectual exercise in the study of his bees.

I had not, I confess, seen as much of my old friend as I would have liked and it was, then, with the greater pleasure that I realised that late September offered me the opportunity to spend a week or two in his company.

On a Friday afternoon towards the end of that month I travelled down to Fulworth. As I jumped down from the station trap outside Holmes' villa, I saw the tall figure of my friend's housekeeper awaiting me by the gate. As always, her thick silver hair was drawn back under an old-fashioned white cap, and her faded blue eyes twinkled as she welcomed me.

'How is he, Martha?' I asked.

'Mizter 'Olmes?' she said. 'Why, doctor, he's right as nine-pence. He smokes too much and he sits too late with his books and papers and sometimes he forgets his dinner when he's with his old bees, but he's all right. He won't say it, of course, but he has been looking forward to you visiting.'

In the evening Holmes and I strolled on the cliff top near the villa, while the great bulk of the Sussex Downs darkened behind us and the sinking sun turned the Channel tide to gold where it broke on the shingle beach below. Fresh from a busy summer in the city I readily understood Holmes' retreat to this beautiful spot.

After dark we returned to a simple supper, and sat late, either side of the small fire set by Martha to defeat the evening chill, while Holmes' pipe was filled and refilled and we reminded each other of episodes that we had shared, or Holmes described to me adventures in which I had had no part.

My holiday mood was firmly established when I rose, rather later than earlier, the next morning, to find my host, still wearing the familiar dressing-gown, seated at the breakfast table. A drift of newspapers littered the floor at his feet.

'Good morning, Holmes,' I said, gesturing towards the papers. 'I see that you have not abandoned all your old habits, then?'

'Once again, Watson, you put your finger on the point,' he

replied, extricating the toast-rack from beneath a newspaper and handing it across. 'This is purely habit – at the most a theoretical exercise. Once the public prints were my daily study, or at least, the criminal intelligence and the personal advertisements. Frequently they gave me a hint as to whose foot we could expect to hear upon our stair at Baker Street. In addition, they were an invaluable source of information on the follies, vices and misfortunes of mankind, a veritable encyclopaedia of humanity for a consulting detective. Now they serve merely to remind me of the world that I have abandoned for the smaller, but infinitely more civilised world of the apiarist.'

'Well,' said I, buttering my toast, 'what does your theoretical survey yield in the way of cases that might once have come our way?'

'Very little, Watson, very little. Once I believed that my absences from London caused unhealthy excitement in criminal circles but, by contrast, my retirement seems to have dulled them entirely. The political writers debate whether our new battleship and the *Entente* with France will secure the peace of Europe, Scotland Yard announces a completely predictable arrest in the Margate investment swindle, and the husband of a lady in Tunbridge Wells left home last Thursday and has not been seen since. Meanwhile, in Nottinghamshire, a carpenter has confessed that he was the East End murderer of the eighties, which of course he was not.'

'Is there no further news of the derailment in Lincolnshire?' I enquired, for the calamity that had overtaken the night mail to Scotland was still very fresh in the public mind.

'None – or none that makes any further sense of the matter. What is more, my expertise in railway matters extends only to a knowledge of routes and the ability to consult a timetable. The Board of Trade enquiry will no doubt establish the cause.'

'It seems to me', I said, 'that Tunbridge Wells is no great distance from here. Can you really be sure that we shall not be consoling a tearful lady with a missing husband before breakfast is done?'

'No, Watson, I regret to say that I cannot. There are still those who manage to find out my retreat and try to avail themselves of my services, but if that lady were to do so I would have to present to her conclusions that are obvious from the newspaper accounts, namely that her errant husband has another love, most probably in Wales and almost certainly a schoolteacher by profession.'

'Really, Holmes!' I protested, but he cut me short with a raised hand.

'Enough, Watson!' he chuckled. 'You know my methods, and when you read the accounts you may check my conclusions for yourself. What is more, nothing would tempt me back to my old career on any but the most temporary basis. I am entirely devoted to my little makers of sweetness, and I suggest that we now devote ourselves to breakfast,' with which he removed the cover from a dish of kippers.

Breakfast done, we took ourselves once more to the cliff top and from there, by a steeply winding path, down to the shingle beach that skirts the coast for some miles in that part of Sussex.

It was a perfect September day of clear sunlight, with a high, cloudless sky. For an hour we trod the pebbles lazily, Holmes occasionally stooping to pick up a sea-smoothed stone or a minute shell and expatiate on the geology or biology of the sea-shore. The Channel sparkled under the sun and across its horizon small boats went about their errands. It was, I thought, an auspicious beginning to a holiday.

We had turned back in our walk and had almost retraced our footsteps to the bottom of the cliff path when we heard a shrill voice calling out, 'Mizter 'Olmes! Mizter 'Olmes!'

Tumbling and slithering down the steep path came a small boy, breathlessly calling my friend's name. As we drew nearer we could see that it was one of Martha's multitudinous nephews. Reaching the shingle he jogged towards us, then fell on his knees in front of us, trying to deliver his message and recover his breath simultaneously, with no great success.

'Now, Bobby,' said Holmes, bending over the child, 'breathe first and speak afterwards!'

Recovered in wind the boy scrambled to his feet. 'Mizter 'Olmes,' he said, 'Auntie do say as you should come quick. There's four gentlemen up at the house as is come to see you urgent. They've come all the way from London – in their own special railway train!' and his eyes widened at the recital of this miraculous tale.

11

'Thank you, Bobby,' said Holmes. 'Now run along back to your aunt and tell her that I shall be home as quickly as may be.'

As the boy ran off Holmes turned to me and raised one eyebrow quizzically. 'It seems, Watson,' he said, 'that your remarks at breakfast were premonitory, but I confess I do not see why anyone should wish to consult me about the accident to the Scottish Mail!'

2

THE PLYMOUTH EXPRESS

'I am Sherlock Holmes,' announced my friend, as we entered the drawing-room of his villa.

His four visitors rose from their seats as one man. I had become enough of a countryman in less than twenty-four hours to see how incongruous their dark City clothes and tall hats looked in the sunlit rural room. The oldest of them, a tall, distinguished-looking gentleman, began to introduce himself.

'Mr Holmes, I am Henry Borrowclere and these gentlemen are –' but Holmes cut him short with a gesture.

'Forgive me, Mr Borrowclere. It may save a good deal of time if you permit me to ask at the outset why on earth you and your colleagues believe that I can throw any light on the fate of the Edinburgh Mail?'

Borrowclere looked as dumbfounded as I had been minutes earlier, and one of his companions muttered, 'Extraordinary!'

'Come now,' said Holmes, 'it is not often that applicants for my assistance arrive in groups of four. It is more usually a single police officer or some individual who may or may not be accompanied by a friend or a solicitor. A group whose dress and bearing proclaim them to be City gentlemen implies a committee or a company. That you arrived at our tiny station in a special train bespeaks both extreme urgency and some influence in the sphere of railways. Nothing, I imagine, more concerns railway operators at the moment than the unexplained fate of the night mail to Edinburgh. Therefore I repeat my question – what makes you believe that I can be of assistance?'

Borrowclere glanced nervously at me and Holmes intercepted the look.

'This is my friend Dr Watson, without whom you might not

have known of me. You may speak freely in front of him, and I warn you, gentlemen, that, though you merely trespass on my retirement, you interrupt my friend at the beginning of a long-awaited holiday!'

Borrowclere looked uncomfortable. 'Mr Holmes, we are too well aware that you have retired from your practice and we apologise to you both for our unpardonable rudeness in arriving without warning. Nevertheless, the matter is of such importance to all of us that we dared not risk a rebuff before we had put our case to you. Between us we speak for two railway companies, and I can assure you that we can and will make any recompense you suggest for disturbing your retirement. As to Dr Watson, we can only apologise again for disturbing his holiday.'

'Two companies?' queried Holmes.

One of Borrowclere's companions stepped forward. 'Mr Borrowclere is from the Great Northern Railway and is concerned with the Edinburgh Mail. I am George Jesson of the London and South-Western Railway Company and this is my colleague, Radley. We have joined forces with the Northern because a nearly identical disaster struck one of our own express trains only a few weeks ago. The results were even worse and in neither case does there seem to be any sensible explanation.'

Holmes turned from them and stared out of the bay window at the sunlit sea. Borrowclere regarded my friend's back with an expression of dismay. 'Do not send us away lightly, Mr Holmes,' he said quietly. 'We are talking about the deaths of more than forty people.'

Holmes swung back to face him. 'You had better be seated, gentlemen, while I hear your story. Mark you, though – I make no promise of assistance! Watson, our visitors have travelled early from London. Pray be so good as to ring the bell and see if Martha can provide refreshment.'

When tea had been served it was Jesson who began the tale.

'The first of these episodes occurred less than three months ago, on the last night of June. The South-Western has a mail and passenger express that meets the New York liners at Plymouth.'

'So that urgent mail and hurried passengers may be disembarked and travel on to London by rail, yes,' interrupted Holmes.

14

'Quite so. Now it is usually a small, light train, as it does not need to carry much and its purpose is to reach London quickly. On the night in question it had only five carriages – a brake van, three first-class carriages and a further brake van at the rear which was also a kitchen. There was to be only one stop between Plymouth and London, at Temple Combe.'

'On the border of Somersetshire and Wiltshire?'

'The same. That was merely an engine stop, so that an express engine could be substituted for the one that had come from Plymouth. The express engine, Number 421, was waiting there with a fresh driver and fireman when the train arrived.'

'Was the train punctual at Temple Combe?'

'She was in good time. If you have travelled our line you will know that it runs through some fairly rugged country, but she was in Temple Combe about one minute before her time. The engines were changed with no difficulty and the new driver took her out on what should have been a straight run through to Waterloo.'

'Were the new driver and fireman experienced? Forgive me – I am aware of the long apprenticeships served by locomotive men – I meant to ask if these two knew the route and the engine well?'

'Yes, indeed. Both Driver Robbins and Fireman Gadd were reliable and experienced, and Robbins knew the route well. They went slowly from Temple Combe, and they were about four minutes late at Dinton, about twenty miles on, but then they seem to have accelerated to a tremendous speed, some seventy miles an hour, and kept that up all the way to the wreck.'

'Which occurred where?'

'At Salisbury, Mr Holmes, about eight miles again from Dinton. It was just before two in the morning when she whistled at Salisbury up signal box, and then she just tore on through into Salisbury.'

'What brought about the wreck?'

'There is a curve at Salisbury, at either end. Coming from east or west there is a speed restriction of thirty miles an hour. Robbins knew he must slacken speed well before entering the west curve.'

Jesson paused, as though uncertain how to continue. 'What happened?' asked Holmes.

'Radley visited next day. I think perhaps he can describe the result better than I.'

Radley leaned forward in his chair and clasped his hands together. 'Despite their fearful speed when they entered the western curve, by some miracle they actually held to the rails right through the station itself, but the eastern curve was their undoing. She was flung from the rails there and smashed into the rear of a milk train that was passing on the down line. As the express overturned, its carriages were completely destroyed, as well as five vans of the milk train. Forty yards of rails were ripped out of the ground. In some places the ground was scored to a depth of several feet.'

He shuddered and sipped from his tea.

'And how many died?' asked Holmes softly.

'Twenty-eight, Mr Holmes,' replied Jesson. 'The driver and fireman, of course, twenty-four out of forty-eight passengers, the guard of the milk train and the fireman of an engine that was standing nearby. Twenty-eight altogether.'

There was silence for some moments while my friend sat, apparently sunk in thought. Then he raised his head.

'I take it that the express engine was very badly damaged?'

'Not so badly as one might expect,' said Radley. 'We were able to take her for repair on her own wheels. Why do you ask?'

'Was it possible to determine whether the unfortunate Robbins had made any attempt to slow down or stop on the approach to Salisbury?'

'That is part of the mystery, Mr Holmes. The regulator had been shut down, to begin slowing her down, but the vacuum brake was still off.'

Holmes drew a long breath. 'Forgive the question,' he said, 'but is there any suggestion that Robbins or Gadd was unwell, or had taken liquor?'

'No, sir! The company is, of course, very strict on the point, but Robbins and Gadd spoke with the staff at Temple Combe. They say that both were sober and in a good state of health and mind before they left.'

'A final question,' said Holmes, 'but again, one that may be a little delicate for the South-Western Railway. You are not the only company supplying expresses to meet the boats at Plymouth. The Great Western has such a service, I believe?'

'Yes, Mr Holmes,' said Jesson. 'What do you imply?'

'I imply nothing, Mr Jesson, but if the business is one of getting passengers and mail to London as quickly as possible, is it not possible that regulations are ignored for the sake of speed, or that a particularly hurried passenger might tip a driver for that reason?'

'Everything is possible, Mr Holmes, but we make it a very serious matter for a driver to be ahead of his time in London, so there is no encouragement of that kind of thing.'

'What is more,' added Radley, 'Driver Robbins had no such intention. At Temple Combe the staff remarked on the boat train arriving early and Robbins said that he wouldn't get into Waterloo before his time for fear of being disciplined.'

'So,' said Holmes, 'we have an experienced crew on a familiar route. The weather – what was the weather like?'

'It was a clear summer night.'

'A fit, sober and experienced crew, a well-known route, fine weather, and no apparent mechanical difficulties – yet Driver Robbins ignored the speed restriction at Salisbury. Was his whistle at the up signal box a normal signal?'

'No, sir,' said Radley. 'He held the whistle down all the way through to the wreck.'

'Did he indeed?' said Holmes. 'Watson, this matter begins to interest me. Ask Martha to replenish the tea, then Mr Borrowclere can tell us about the Edinburgh Mail.'

3

THE SCOTTISH MAIL

'The fate of the Edinbugh Mail was, in all respects, similar to the disaster at Salisbury,' said Borrowclere. 'The train had left King's Cross at a quarter to nine on the evening of 19th September. It was carrying both mail and passengers and was to stop at Peterborough, Grantham and Doncaster on its way.'

'Was this also a small train?' asked Holmes.

'Not so small as the Plymouth boat train, no. Our train had twelve carriages, two of them sleeping cars, with three brake vans and the mail coach at the front. There was no difficulty at Peterborough, where there was an engine change. Number 276, a relatively new locomotive, was waiting to take the train on.'

'Was there a change of the driving crew?'

'Yes, Mr Holmes. Driver Fleetwood and Fireman Talbot were to take her on. Fleetwood had driven for eighteen years, the last two years solely on Number 276. Talbot was a bright young man who had served a premium apprenticeship at Doncaster. He was working under the District Locomotive Superintendent, firing various types of engine to study their performance.'

'Were both familiar with the route?'

'Entirely – in fact, they had worked it the previous night.'

'I must ask you, as I asked Mr Jesson, were the men healthy and sober?'

'They spoke with the staff at Peterborough. All of them say that Fleetwood and Talbot were normal and sober, Mr Holmes. They changed engines and left with no difficulty.'

'With no stop ahead until Grantham?' queried Holmes.

'No stop until Grantham at eleven o'clock,' repeated Borrowclere. 'Just before eleven the mails were made ready at Grantham on the down platform. At Grantham South, the first signal box coming into Grantham, the distant signal was set at "Caution".'

'Why was that?'

'At three minutes before eleven a goods train was to cross the down main line. It was crossing from the up Nottingham line to the up main line. It had, thereby, to cross the down main line, the line on which the express would arrive.'

'Forgive me, Mr Borrowclere: I am becoming confused by your use of "up" and "down".'

'The fault is mine, Mr Holmes. In railway usage the "up main line" is the line towards London. Thus the King's Cross train was expected on the "down main line", the line from London. The north signal box had all its down main signals at "Danger". The south box had its distant signal at "Caution" to warn the express driver that Grantham Station was not clear for it, that the points were set to allow the goods train to cross.'

'Was there any reason why Driver Fleetwood may not have seen that signal? What was the state of the weather?'

'It was dark, Mr Holmes, with occasional showers of rain, but visibility was clear and the red lamps were in order. We know of no reason why he should not have seen them.'

'But it seems he did not,' said Holmes.

'He must have done,' said Borrowclere. 'But, having seen them, he ignored them. While the goods was crossing, the night inspector and the postmen were waiting on the down platform. They heard a train coming and, as it flashed past them, they saw the mail van on it and realised that the express had ignored the "Caution" signal and was running on through the "Danger" signal.'

'At what speed did it enter Grantham?'

'Inspector Pyle says forty miles an hour, but others say more. Nevertheless it stayed on the rails and found a way on to the Nottingham line. It even negotiated the first curve, but the second curve derailed the tender. It tore out the parapet of an underbridge for more than sixty yards, then toppled over it. As it did so, it wrenched the locomotive from the rails, so that it slewed broadside across the track and the first three carriages crashed into it.'

'Were those passenger carriages?'

'Fortunately not, Mr Holmes. They were brake vans and the

mail coach, but the next six coaches hurtled down the embankment beyond the bridge. Only the last three remained upright.'

'The driver and fireman did not survive?'

'No, sir. They must have died instantaneously. After the impact the wreck took fire, both the wreckage on the line and that below.'

'The upper wreckage igniting from the firebox, I assume, and the lower from the carriage gaslights?'

'Indeed, Mr Holmes.' Borrowclere paused. 'Altogether fourteen persons died in the wreck: the driver and fireman, a postal clerk and eleven passengers.'

'So,' said Holmes, 'once more we have a fit and experienced crew, familiar with their route, and sober, yet they ran their train into danger, ignoring the warning signals. Was there any attempt to slow or stop the engine?'

'It was impossible to tell. The engine was so badly damaged we could not determine the position of the regulator or brake lever. There is one other thing, Mr Holmes.'

'What is that?'

'We do not know at all what to make of it. The signalman at Grantham South, Signalman Day, says he saw the driver and fireman as the train ran past his box.'

'And what were they doing?'

'Nothing, Mr Holmes. Day insists that they were standing each side of the footplate, staring ahead through the spectacle glasses, the little ports in the front of the cab.'

'And he is sure of this?'

'He has been questioned and questioned again, because it does not seem to make any sense, but he insists that is what he saw, Mr Holmes.'

'Then it must be,' said Holmes. 'Or, in the absence of other data, we must take account of his. Tell me, Mr Borrowclere, should the Edinburgh Mail have whistled at the signal box – and did it?'

'No, Mr Holmes, it did not. It should have done, but it did not.'

Holmes rose and paced the room. 'So the Plymouth Express whistled when it was not expected to do so, but the Edinburgh Mail did not whistle when it should have done. I confess, gentlemen, your problems interest me.'

He turned his back again, and for a long time gazed out of the window. When he turned back he spoke as though there had been no interruption in the conversation.

'But I ask you again, gentlemen – why do you believe that I can assist you? My study has been crime and that is the least likely explanation here. Why would a criminal wreck an express train? To kill? To rob? To destroy? No, gentlemen. Were there some consignment to destroy, some passenger to murder, aboard a train, a wreck such as you describe would be a most unreliable means to accomplish those ends. In the worst of your instances – in the Plymouth boat train – half of the passengers survived, and no doubt a good deal of luggage and mail. There is no way in which a criminal could guarantee the destruction of a particular item or person in a train wreck.'

He paced the floor again. 'If robbery were the motive, the converse argument applies – there is no way to guarantee the survival of the item you wish to steal, let alone to ensure that the train crashes at a particular spot. No, you are almost certainly not dealing with crime, and I cannot see that my skills will assist you.'

'Mr Holmes,' said Radley, earnestly, 'not all of the matters which Dr Watson here has recorded had criminal explanations, surely? We believe that there is no man in Britain better equipped to look into these two dreadful accidents and tell us what caused them.'

'It is of the gravest importance to both our companies,' said Borrowclere. 'The loss of so many lives is dreadful in any case, but usually there is an explanation, some fault in some system can be determined as the cause, and measures taken to prevent any recurrence. Here we have two inexplicable tragedies within a few weeks. We cannot tell the public and the Board of Trade that it will never happen again. If we do not know what occurred at Salisbury and at Grantham we cannot say but that it may happen to our companies or to another operator tomorrow – at Cardiff, or at Carlisle, at Dover, or anywhere. The public will lose confidence in rail travel completely, and with reason!'

His companion spoke for the first time. 'The public is suspicious, Mr Holmes. The most alarming tales are circulating. People are saying that poor Fleetwood was drunk, or that he had gone insane. They even say that Fleetwood and his fireman were seen struggling with each other on the footplate. If these stories are not scotched by a realistic explanation, then the railway's day will be over in this country and we shall all be condemned to travel in draughty, stinking motor cars!'

'Gentlemen,' said Holmes, 'I warned you from the first that I am three years retired, and I am not convinced that a consulting detective is what you need. I must tell you –'

Borrowclere had drawn a paper from his pocket and now placed it in my friend's hand. 'Before you turn us away, Mr Holmes, please read that note. It is from the person who suggested that we consult you.'

Holmes unfolded the document and, after a glance at its contents, passed it to me. The sheet of white bond bore the embossed address of the Diogenes Club in Pall Mall and the previous day's date, together with a few lines in a bold and instantly recognisable hand:

My dear Sherlock,
Forgive this intrusion upon your deserved retirement.
   My friend Borrowclere and his colleagues seem to have serious problems and I have taken the liberty of suggesting that you may be able to help them.
   Need I say that I (and His Majesty's Government) will be deeply grateful if you are able to assist my friend?
   Your affectionate brother, M.

I returned the note to Holmes and he folded it into his coat pocket, his lips pursed tightly.

'Very well gentlemen,' he said. 'I shall make such enquiries as seem relevant. It is, as I have said, Watson's holiday, and I insist that he be allowed at least the remainder of the weekend before you remove his host. Mr Radley, is the engine of your boat train back in service?'

'It is completely repaired, sir, but still at the workshops at Nine Elms.'

'If it is possible, I would like to have it at Temple Combe on Tuesday morning, with a crew at least as experienced as Robbins and Gadd. Please make the necessary traffic arrangements so that I may ride with it from Temple Combe to Salisbury.'

22

'I shall see to it immediately,' said Radley, and he and his colleagues looked vastly relieved.

'Now, gentlemen, perhaps you will leave Dr Watson and me to rescue a little of this weekend. I shall be at Plymouth on Monday and will leave word with the South-Western office there to let you know where I may be found. Good-day, gentlemen.'

They rose and took their leave, each expressing his gratitude to Holmes. As their carriage rolled away towards Fulworth I turned to my friend. 'Well, Holmes,' I said, 'what brought about your change of mind?'

'I do not know', he said, 'if it was the curious business of the whistles, or the even more curious involvement of Mycroft. He has no interest that I know of in the reputation of railway companies. Why should he be deeply grateful, I wonder, let alone His Majesty's Government?'

4

THE VANISHING LADY

That Holmes did not travel alone to Plymouth on the following Monday will not surprise my readers. Indeed, I should have been disappointed had he not invited me to join him, for I was not too old to feel the same quickening of the spirit that I had first felt at Baker Street, a quarter of a century before, when some new adventure beckoned.

On Sunday Holmes passed the evening dragging books from the shelves of his study, principally maps and gazetteers. From time to time he scribbled notes, preparing a list of information that he required from the railway companies.

At length he turned to the old commonplace books, in which, as long as I had known him, he had accumulated strange and rare items of criminal lore. He searched through volume after volume, running his forefinger rapidly down the pages, then thrusting the book back into the case and taking another. Now and then he would carry one to the lamp and read for a few minutes, before slamming the volume shut with a snort of impatience.

When he had exhausted the long row of worn volumes he returned to his chair and sat, drumming his fingers on the table, for some minutes.

'There is simply no such thing, Watson!' he ejaculated at last.

'No such thing as what, Holmes?' I enquired.

'Railway crime in this country,' he said. 'I can count on the fingers of one hand the significant crimes associated with our railway system since it first began. There was Pierce and Agar's theft of the Crimea payroll half a century ago, a crime of considerable ingenuity and originality, and what else? The

24

murder of Briggs on the North London Railway in '64, which would already be forgotten if it had not led to the installation of the communication cord, and the death of Isaac Gold on the Brighton line in '81!'

'You are disappointed?' I asked.

'Watson, there is no one who observes the progress of science more closely than the professional criminal. Every invention brings in its wake some new crime – except, it seems, the railway. After three-quarters of a century that great invention has attracted one daring theft and a few pathetic murders. No, Watson, I was right. There is no crime here, only some human or mechanical failure.'

Early the next morning we set out for Plymouth, first telegraphing to Jesson to provide the information that Holmes required. At Waterloo we were met by a clerk with manilla folders and a large roll of maps. He showed us to a reserved compartment and, before the train left, presented us with a pair of handsomely engraved *laissez-passers*, valid for travel upon any British railway.

As we rolled westwards Holmes busied himself with the bundle of documents, unrolling maps of the railway system and diagrams of stations until the floor and seats of our compartment were covered in them.

While he peered intently at maps and consulted lists, I watched the changing landscape. Gradually the heathland that borders London on the west gave way to the lush, well-watered valleys of Hampshire and the rolling green of Wiltshire. Soon the rutted cart-tracks in the fields began to reveal the raw, red soil of the West Country and by late afternoon we were pulling into Plymouth.

The station master himself met us there and had us taken to rooms he had engaged at the Golden Hind where, after dinner, we retired to our sitting-room with a bottle of port.

Now my friend directed his attention to one of the manilla folders. It seemed to contain largely typewritten reports and lists, which he compared carefully. After a while he passed me two sheets of paper bearing a list of names and addresses. He took a bundle of documents into his own hands.

'If you will assist me, Watson,' he said. 'I have passed you a list of passengers on the Plymouth train, as compiled after the

25

event. Those with crosses against them are the names of the dead. I have here the depositions taken from the survivors. Let me read their names and addresses and be so good as to check them against your list.'

From each deposition he read the maker's name and address, until he had been through them all, and as he read each one I found the same name and particulars in the list I held until he had turned over the last page in his sheaf.

'Well, Watson?' he enquired.

'You seem to be short of one deposition, Holmes. Apart from the dead, and the names you have given me, there is one name you have not read out.'

'Precisely!' he ejaculated. 'There is no statement here from Mr Jonathan Y. Samuel of New York, nor does your list show any address but in care of the Victoria Hotel, Northumberland Avenue.'

'Quite right,' I said, and looked through the list again. I imagined the hideous scene of carnage at Salisbury on that midsummer night and reflected on my own battlefield experiences. 'Are you sure there has been no confusion between the living and the dead?'

'Count those with crosses, Watson. There are only twenty-four.'

'Surely, Holmes, if Mr Samuel was at the Victoria Hotel there was no reason why the company could not obtain a statement from him?'

'Quite so, and it is a simple matter to check. Kindly pass me my writing-case and ring for the boy.'

Once the hotel's boy had departed with a 'Reply paid' telegram, Holmes relaxed. His former intensity and impatience melted away and we fell once more to rehearsing old adventures while we finished the port. I had seen the phenomenon many times in the early stages of a case. From the senseless ravel of the two railway wrecks Holmes had succeeded in teasing out a loose end. Now, if I knew my friend, he would pull it steadily until the whole matter began to unwind.

We were about to turn in when the boy returned with a reply. The manager of the Victoria confirmed that no Jonathan Y. Samuel had been there.

'So our passenger from New York gave the company a false address!' I said.

'You jump to a conclusion, Watson,' said Holmes. 'Mr Samuel may well have stayed at the Victoria, but since the name he gave the railway company was almost certainly an alias, he may have changed his name again.'

'Why do you say the name is false?'

'Evidently he sought to avoid contact by giving that address, in which case he may well have added a false name. Furthermore, Watson, I suspect our mysterious traveller of a degree of wit. What do you imagine is signified by the middle Y?'

I confessed myself nonplussed and Holmes smiled. 'Why, Yankee, of course, Watson!'

'Surely there is no such name – even among Americans?'

'His first name, Watson, is the old nickname by which we called our American cousins, and his surname equates with a certain "Uncle Sam". Might not the middle initial indicate our present term for his fellow countrymen?'

I shook my head, wondering, as often, at my friend's extraordinary mental processes.

We broke our fast early and proceeded at once to the London and South-Western offices, where an obliging clerk found for us the record of passengers booked from the liner *New York* on to the boat train on 30th June. Jonathan Y. Samuel was not among them. His place in the list was taken by a Miss Eileen Neagle, also of New York.

As we made our way to the shipping company's office I pondered on this latest discovery.

'Holmes,' I said, 'we seem to have a lady on the American liner who booked on the boat train and disappeared, while her place was taken by a man with a false name and address who also disappeared after the catastrophe. Have you formed any theory as to what this has to do with the two crashes?'

'It is a primary error', said Holmes, 'to believe that items of information found in close proximity are necessarily related, and it is another to speculate too far in advance of one's data. All of this may have nothing to do with derailed expresses. It may have to do with romantic intrigues, international espionage or mere personal idiosyncrasies. For all we know at present, Mr

Samuel may be the missing husband from Tunbridge Wells and Miss Neagle his light of love.'

The shipping company confirmed that Miss Neagle had indeed been a passenger from New York and had booked on to the boat train. No 'Mr Samuel' had been on the liner or on the train.

We were climbing into a cab outside the office when the shipping clerk who had attended us dashed out of the office carrying a small envelope.

'Mr Holmes,' he said, 'if you're looking into the affairs of Miss Neagle, this may assist, perhaps. I had forgot all about it, but a colleague put me in mind. This telegram came here for the lady on that night, but it was too late, the train had already gone.'

Sherlock Holmes thanked him and sat back in the cab as we pulled away, tearing open the yellow envelope. He read its contents and smiled.

'Well, Watson, at least we have the answer to your question. Miss Neagle and Mr Samuel, if either of them really exists, are very likely to be connected with our enquiries,' and he passed me the telegram.

It had been sent from London late on 30th June, and its message was brief.

MISS EILEEN NEAGLE
LINER NEW YORK AT PLYMOUTH
MR SAMUEL IS URGENTLY AWAITED AT THE BARREL STOP
HE MUST NOT BE LATE STOP M

It left me none the wiser, and I admitted my puzzlement to Holmes. 'It shows that Miss Neagle and Mr Samuel are connected and that he had an appointment in London of some urgency to the writer, who was apparently expecting him at an inn or hotel called The Barrel, but how that links them with our enquiry I do not see.'

Holmes laughed. 'The Barrel, Watson, is almost certainly not a public hostelry. It is a transparently simple code for that most exclusive of Pall Mall clubs patronised by my brother – the Diogenes Club, named for a philosopher who dwelt in a barrel. If further confirmation were needed, it bears his characteristically brief signature. I really think that, when we have completed our business in the West Country, we must seek out Mycroft and ask him the nature of his interest in this affair!'

5

PREPARATIONS FOR AN EXPERIMENT

Radley waited for us on the platform at Temple Combe and took us for luncheon at the village inn. Once we were served he asked Holmes what, precisely, he required of the railway company.

'We have brought Number 421 here,' he said, 'with as good a crew as we can find, but we cannot make detailed traffic arrangements until we know exactly what you wish to do.'

'I wish', said Holmes, 'to travel on the footplate of Number 421, the entire distance from here to Salisbury, but as slowly as possible. I have studied the plans of the line and stations which you provided, and I now wish to examine the route in detail, so that I may see what Driver Robbins saw, or perhaps what he failed to see. For that reason I would also like to do it at night and in as near as possible the same conditions. Tonight looks like being equally clear, if not so warm. I think we shall have as near a simulation as we can construct.'

'Then I suggest', said Radley, 'that I arrange for Number 421 to leave here immediately after tonight's boat train has passed. I will telegraph the necessary traffic arrangements so that you will have a clear line to Salisbury.'

'Excellent!' said Holmes. 'Now tell me, are there any staff at Temple Combe this afternoon who were here on the night in question?'

'I thought you might wish to question them yourself, Mr Holmes, and I have arranged that they will all be at the station today.'

After luncheon we repaired to the station, where Radley introduced us to the men who were there on the fatal night, before commandeering the telegraph to make arrangements for our experiment.

Holmes pursued with Mr Furze, the night inspector, and with a shunter called Mullet, his questions concerning the health and sobriety of the engine-men, but they were emphatic in their opinion that both men were well and sober. It was evident that they were speaking the truth, not merely defending the reputations of dead colleagues.

Shunter Mullet had spoken to Robbins about speed, and Holmes pressed him on the point. 'Now, Mr Mullet, have you never heard of a boat train driver accepting a little something from a passenger in a hurry?'

'I dare say I has, sir, maybe more than once, sir, but not Robbins, sir. He wasn't that kind of a man. We was stood on this platform when the train came in and I said to him, "She's running well to time," because she was a minute or two ahead. "I dare say she is," he said to me, "but I shan't get into Waterloo before my time, else I shall have to go up and see the Governor." No, sir, he wasn't a-going to run her fast.'

We climbed on to the footplate of Number 421, where she stood on a side rail, and Inspector Furze brought to us the men with whom we would ride that night. Driver Prust was a stocky man in his fifties, with a thick, greying moustache, while Fireman Tarrant was a tall, lean man of forty or so. Together they demonstrated their working practices and showed Holmes how the engine was controlled when in motion. When they had done, Prust asked, 'What exactly do you want of us tonight, sir?'

'Dr Watson and I will ride with you and I want you to keep us travelling at a slow, steady pace from here to Salisbury. The doctor and I will watch from the sides for anything that strikes us as unusual. In the mean time we must rely on you good fellows to maintain the engine and to let us know if you become aware of anything out of the ordinary. I believe you know this route well?'

'Bless you, sir,' said Tarrant, 'Driver Prust here can tell you if a rail has gone loose from one journey to the next, just by the feel of it!'

'Excellent!' said Holmes. 'That is precisely the sort of thing I had in mind. Now, the doctor and I will meet you here a little before the boat train passes tonight.'

'You'll want to wrap up warm, gentlemen, if you'm watching

from the side all the way to Salisbury,' said Driver Prust. 'You'll be main cold else.'

'Thank you for your warning,' said Holmes, as we swung ourselves down from the footplate.

Walking back to the inn I asked Holmes what it was that he expected to see. 'I expect to see nothing!' he snapped. 'To expect to see something is to be more than half-way to seeing it, even when it is not there – to say nothing of not seeing what is there. Tonight we shall look to see if there is anything along the line which should not be there, or anything absent which should be there. That, Watson, is observation!'

Arrived at the inn, Holmes explained our requirements to the landlady, apologising for any inconvenience.

'Now, don't you worry, Mr Holmes,' she said. 'Mr Furze has told me how you'm here to do an experiment about that awful train crash, and if you can do something as stops things like that, I'm only too pleased to be of service. All those poor people – it fair makes you frightened to go on the trains, it do so. Now, what'll you be wanting, Mr Holmes?'

'We should first like to take tea in your back parlour and then, if we may, to have the use of it for the rest of the evening. Unhappily our experiment cannot begin until the boat train has passed through, which means we shall keep you late. Might we also trouble you for a little cold supper later on?'

'That's no trouble, Mr Holmes. Oh, if my Albert were only here to meet you! He's a great one for reading, my Albert is, and the vicar gives him magazines with your stories in, doctor,' and she favoured me with a smile. 'He's off visiting with his sister in Bath, but you wait till I tell him I've had Mr Sherlock Holmes and the great Dr Watson right here, in our own back parlour!'

She bustled away to prepare our tea and Holmes turned to me with a raised eyebrow. 'It seems, Watson, that a reputation for writing sensational accounts of my investigations counts for more in rural Somerset than that of the mere criminal agent who solved them – the "great Dr Watson" indeed!'

After tea we sat in the parlour, Holmes still poring over his bundle of maps and plans while I studied a detailed map of our route to Salisbury. Finally he drew out the list bearing the name of Jonathan Y. Samuel and the telegram to Miss Neagle.

He laid them side by side on the table and sat smoking his pipe in silence with the fingers of his left hand resting on the two documents.

At last the sounds of customers in the front bar died away and we heard our landlady shoot the bolt of the front door. Some fifteen minutes later a tap at the parlour door announced her arrival with our supper of sandwiches. When she had served us, she poked up the fire.

'Now, gentlemen, if there's nothing more I can do for you, I'll be off to my bed. If you'll be good enough to see to the lamp before you go, you can go out by the side door.'

'I fear we put you to extra trouble,' I said.

'Not at all, doctor! Mr Furze says the railway'll pay for any trouble and, anyway, my Albert'd never forgive me if I didn't treat you right! Besides, I've had experimenters here before, you know.'

'Really?' I said.

'Oh yes! We had a gentleman in midsummer, come from London one day with a great brass telescope with legs that folded up. Said he'd come to see a special face of the moon.'

'An astronomer?' I asked.

'That's it, doctor. 'Course, he wasn't as famous as you and Mr Holmes, but my Albert said he'd seen his picture in the magazines and he was famous for something else. He said as Temple Combe was the best place in the world to watch the moon that night. He used this parlour, just like you, then he had a telegram telling him just where to go and see the moon and off he went. Still, I musn't be keeping you from your supper. Goodnight, gentlemen!'

We bade her goodnight and settled to our supper, lingering over it until it was time to start for the station. Remembering Driver Prust's warning, Holmes had his ulster and a cloth cap, with a wollen scarf about his face, while I had a sound tweed overcoat and a soft cap.

As the parlour clock chimed our appointed time, Holmes turned down the lamp and held open the door.

'Come, Watson,' he said.

6

TERROR ON THE FOOTPLATE

However long it may be before this memoir reaches the public, I dare say that there will still be no man or boy among my readers who has never longed to be an engine driver. Certainly in my own childhood, my brother and I would break off our games and pastimes in the woods and fields at the whistle of an approaching train, and dash to the line side to wave at the engine-men, each of us imagining ourselves on the footplate, controlling the great snorting, smoking juggernaut. So it was that, when Holmes and I mounted the footplate of Number 421 that night, I felt a certain pleasure at the prospect of actually riding with the crew of an express engine.

For those who have never ridden on the footplate, it may assist if I explain that it is, in essence, a large fireplace. At the rear of the engine's boiler is a bulkhead, in the lower centre of which the firebox door opens, much like a larger version of a kitchen range. Above and to either side of the firebox are two forward-facing windows – the same 'spectacle' glasses through which the Grantham signalman had seen the crew of the Edinburgh Mail staring. Between these windows is a daunting array of pipes, levers, valves and cocks, with which the driver regulates his engine, among them being various gauge dials to inform him of the state of steam pressure, water and so on. The whole is roofed over in metal, with small portholes in either side, just forward of the entries.

To the rear of the footplate lies the coal tender. Little concession to the comfort of the engine-men is made, consisting merely of a small seat for driver and fireman, to the left and right of the firebox respectively. If I have given any idea that the crew's working area is a large one, let me remind you that, since the abandonment of the sensible old 'broad gauge', the wheels of a railway train are only four feet and eight inches apart. There was, therefore, little space on the footplate of Number 421 once all four of us had assembled.

'Now then,' said Holmes, 'if Driver Prust and his colleague are to have room to work their engine without interference, you and I, Watson, must make ourselves as small as possible. I suggest that I take the left-hand side – the "driver's side" I believe you call it, Mr Prust? – and watch over the side; while Dr Watson does the same on the right. In that fashion we shall get as good a view of the line and surrounding countryside as we may, while leaving most of the footplate to the operators.'

Holmes had lowered the ear-flaps of his cap and tied them beneath his chin. He was winding his scarf about his face and I was turning my cap backwards, in motoring fashion, when we all heard the rumble of the approaching boat train. Holmes lifted his watch from his pocket. 'Good!' he said. 'The boat train is well to her time. Now let us take up our places and be on the line as soon as we may. We must not delay the business of the London and South-Western Railway more than is necessary!' and he turned and leaned over the side of the cab.

Settling my cap firmly on my head, I too turned from the warm interior of the cab, smelling of oil and Welsh coal together with a curious underlying sweet scent, and took my place at the side of the cab.

Soon we saw the Plymouth train drawing out of Temple Combe and, as its sound faded in the distance, the points ahead of us groaned and clacked into a new position, to release us. Driver Prust stood to his complicated controls and with three great breaths from Number 421 we rolled slowly on to the main line.

The first part of our journey was so uneventful as to be tedious. For mile after mile Driver Prust kept the engine at an even pace, while Holmes and I peered out from the sides of the cab. It was, as Holmes had predicted, a clear night, lit by a bright moon, and the surrounding countryside and the line ahead were easy to see, but as each mile passed I saw nothing that struck me as irregular in either. Indeed, as the night went on I found it more and more difficult to maintain my watch. The steady beat of Number 421's wheels on the track, sometimes augmented by

35

the rhythmic grating of Fireman Tarrant's long shovel plying coal, became soporific, and only the cold air beating on my face, together with the spatters of grit from the funnel, enabled me to stay awake.

We had completed the greater part of our journey and I had begun to look forward to a warm bed in Salisbury, when it occurred to me that something was changing. Accustomed as I had become to the metronomic clacking of our wheels over the rail joints, I failed for some minutes to realise that the tempo was increasing and that we must now be travelling a good deal faster. I thought nothing of it, believing that Holmes had decided that we were learning nothing from our observations and had told Prust to increase the engine's speed.

I continued to keep watch, as farms and barns, fields and hedges, slipped across the landscape, still with no sign of any irregularity, but from time to time my mind returned to the rhythm of the engine, and after a while I became so convinced that we were now travelling at a high speed that I turned to the interior of the cab to ask why we were accelerating.

To my horror I saw at once that Fireman Tarrant, on the small seat beside me, appeared to be asleep. He was slumped forward with his eyes closed, supported only by the shovel which he still held between his two hands. Across the footplate Driver Prust sprawled on his seat, arms hanging at his sides and a look of idiotic amusement on his face. Holmes' lean back was towards me as he continued to keep his watch from the other side of the cab.

I confess, without shame, that I was profoundly frightened. The engine's speed was now at the least sixty miles an hour, if not more, and I and my friend were in the hands of a crew who appeared to be helplessly drunk.

'Holmes!' I shouted, above the roar of the engine. 'Holmes! We are in great danger!'

He turned into the cab and took in the situation at once. Seizing Driver Prust under the armpits he manhandled him against the tender, leaving him sprawled on top of the coals, while I struggled to follow suit with the dead weight of the fireman.

Once the engine-men were out of the way, Holmes took up a position in front of the firebox, balancing himself against the rocking motion of the floor.

'Holmes!' I cried again. 'What on earth can we do?'

'We might yet jump from the side,' he said, 'but to do so would be to abandon these men to their fate. We must stop the engine. Pray take the whistle handle over your head there and hold it down.'

I grasped for the fireman's whistle handle and jerked it down. Over the rattle and roar of the racing engine a piercing scream split the night. A hot, thick sweat broke out on my brow and, as I watched Holmes surveying the gauges and controls before him, I was fearfully aware that we must now be only a few short miles from our destination. Were we too to end our desperate ride in a welter of shattered metal across the curves at Salisbury Station?

Holmes stepped forward and began to wrestle with one of the control handles on the bulkhead. I moved to assist him, but he waved me back with his free hand. 'The whistle, Watson!' he shouted. 'Keep it sounding!'

With one hand I clung to the side of the cab, while with the other I grasped the whistle handle as for very life. The engine was now reeling on the rails and beyond Holmes I could see the moonlit landscape flashing past in a continuous blur, so great was our speed.

Perspiration streamed from my brow and my vision blurred. My legs weakened at the knees and I very nearly stumbled to the floor. My brain, a moment ago made crystal clear by our desperate predicament, now seemed dulled as if by sleep, and I wondered why my comrade was wrestling with the controls. My hand lost its grip on the whistle handle and I sank on to the fireman's seat.

'Watson!' shouted Holmes. 'The whistle! Sound the whistle!' and I dragged myself upright again to grasp the handle. Now, despite the furious speed of the engine, I seemed to experience everything at a remove. The locomotive noise was muffled and the whistle seemed thin and distant. I forgot our terrifying speed and the proximity of Salisbury Station, and a gust of insane laughter shook me.

With a final wrench at one of the controls, Holmes turned away from them and sprang across the footplate. He removed my nerveless hand from the whistle and turned me against the side of the cab. He held me there, with my face outside the metal screen, while he pulled down the whistle handle.

The wind tore my cap from my head and beat about my face so strongly that at first I could barely breathe. Gradually I recovered my breath, but still found myself weak and dizzy.

When I had gained a little possession of myself, I started up against Holmes' grip. 'The engine, Holmes!' I panted. 'Can you not stop her?'

He restrained me with a firm hand. 'Listen!' he commanded.

I listened, and slowly I realised that the rhythm of our journey had changed again. Now the clack of the rail joints was slowing beneath us and the engine's pace slackened. Soon we were back to that steady rhythm with which Driver Prust had brought us out of Temple Combe.

'Reach up with your left hand and take the whistle,' said Holmes. 'No! Do not turn into the cab, just hold it from where you are. I must try to apply the brake,' and he crossed the footplate again.

Moments later I was still clinging dizzily to the whistle control when Number 421 shuddered to a halt close to Salisbury West signal box. As soon as the locomotive was at rest I stumbled from the footplate on unsteady legs and vomited violently at the trackside.

THE DEVICE OF A MANIAC

I recovered myself to find Sherlock Holmes standing at my side. 'Watson, old friend, are you all right?' he asked.

I nodded and drew a deep breath of clean night air. 'I feel a little better now, Holmes. Let us see to those poor fellows on the tender.'

The signalman had run down from his cabin and, with his assistance, Holmes lifted Driver Prust and his fireman down to the ground. Once they were comfortably set down, Holmes took the signalman's lantern and examined the faces of the engine-men closely by its light. They seemed to be in a daze or trance, from which the fresh air and the lantern's light were gradually waking them.

Holmes straightened up and turned to me, handing me the lantern. 'If you feel up to it, Watson, be so good as to confirm that these men are not drunk, and let me have your medical opinion on their condition.'

I bent over them and examined them for myself. The blurring of my vision had eased, but my eyes still did not focus readily in the lamp's glare. The men's faces seemed to be darkly flushed, and the smoke smears of their profession were streaked white where profuse sweat had run down their cheeks. The pupils of their eyes were narrowed, and their breathing appeared slower than normal. With Holmes' help I timed the pulses of both men and found each of them to be extremely rapid and irregular.

'Well, Watson?' queried Holmes, as I concluded my examination.

'This is extraordinary, Holmes! These men are certainly not drunk. There is no smell of alcohol about them, but they exhibit all the symptoms of being drugged with something else. I cannot imagine how, but they appear to have been poisoned with some form of opiate!'

'Then your opinion concurs with mine, Watson. Now, here are people coming from the station and it should be possible to move these men to a place where they may be cared for.'

A group of figures had come running along the line from Salisbury Station, some of them with lanterns. As Holmes began to give them directions I sat beside the track, my dizziness and heaviness returning. I recall little more of that night, beyond a stumbling walk along the lineside, assisted by Holmes, and later the jolting of a cab, presumably taking us to our hotel.

My waking the next morning was not the most pleasant. Opening my eyes, even to the dimmed light of a curtained room, was a painful effort, and to find myself in a totally strange bedchamber confused my aching head unbearably. My tongue clove to the roof of my mouth and, even as I lay, I felt the weakness of my limbs. Since the furnishing of the room betokened an hotel, I reached for the bell-cord. At that moment there was a tap at the door.

Without waiting for my summons the door opened to admit Holmes, bearing a cup on a tray.

'Ah, Watson!' he exclaimed. 'Let me wish you good morning!'

I fumbled for the power of speech. 'Holmes!' I said. 'Where in the world are we?'

'Have you forgotten last night's events so soon, Watson? We are at the Duke of Clarence, a respectable and ancient inn in Salisbury, to which we brought you after our adventures on the footplate of Number 421.'

Recollection flooded back, causing an involuntary shudder. I reached for the cup which Holmes offered and the strong, sweet coffee soon quickened my memory.

'Do you feel up to a little breakfast?' enquired Holmes. 'It is already laid in the sitting-room next door and, if it would not overtax you, I would like to ask Radley to join us. I owe both of you some explanation of last night and the servants tell me that poor Radley has been waiting in the parlour downstairs since they first opened the doors this morning.'

Despite my weakness I was eager to hear my friend's conclusions on the extraordinary events of the previous night. 'Give me fifteen minutes, Holmes, and I shall join you and Radley.'

The training of an old campaigner allowed me to keep to my word. A little under fifteen minutes later I entered the sitting-room, where Radley and Holmes sat. Radley sprang up at my entrance.

'Dr Watson!' he exclaimed. 'How are you?'

'This morning I can walk and talk, which is, I think, an improvement on my state last night,' I said. 'How are the engine-men?'

'I have been at the hospital this morning. Both have recovered consciousness, but neither is able to explain how they were overcome on the footplate last night. The doctors tell me that they will make a complete recovery with rest.'

Holmes plied both of us with coffee, which was all that I felt able to take by way of breakfast, and when we were settled, began his narrative.

'I told you, Mr Radley, at Temple Combe, that I had made certain discoveries. At that stage I had discovered that a lady called Miss Eileen Neagle had shipped aboard the *New York* and disembarked at Plymouth. Your company records reveal that she intended to take the boat train to Waterloo, and we know from another source that she had an urgent appointment in London on what I will describe as "government business". The company's records of the dead and the survivors in the catastrophe show that she did not, apparently, travel on the train. Her place appears to have been taken by a Jonathan Y. Samuel, whose name was almost certainly false and whose only address was an hotel at which your agents did not find him.'

'But what have they to do with the derailment?'

'Perhaps nothing, though I believe there is a connection. However, that connection relates to the "government business", and for that reason I cannot reveal my suspicions to you in detail at present. I can, I think, tell you exactly how the tragedy came about, provided I have your word that the information will remain confidential until such time as I release it.'

Radley drew back from the table. 'Mr Holmes,' he said, 'I think you may be asking too much. I have told you how important the resolution of this mystery is to myself and my fellow directors. How can you ask me to keep your findings secret?'

'Mr Radley, what I have discovered leaves no trace of blame for the catastrophe upon the London and South-Western. It does, however, suggest most strongly that the nation's interest is involved. Until I can be sure on that point I must ask you to maintain silence, even to your colleagues.'

'If you say so, Mr Holmes, then I must accept your embargo for the time being.'

'Thank you,' said Holmes. 'Now, gentlemen, you will recall that, from the start, I protested that I had no expertise in railway matters. My criminal studies led me to believe that deliberate interference with trains is almost unknown in Britain, and I found it hard to believe that it might have happened twice within three months. Nevertheless, the testimony of Signalman Day at Grantham, and the curious question of the whistles, had led me to a theory as to what might have happened had the derailments been the result of crime.'

'And were you correct?' asked Radley, but Holmes continued, ignoring the question.

'I carried out last night's experiment in the hope that some more ordinary cause would reveal itself. In fact, by an accident, the experiment revealed to me not only that the Plymouth boat train was deliberately derailed, but also the method.'

'But how?' asked Radley and I, simultaneously.

'By the cunning device of a maniac – by this!' said Holmes, and drew from his pocket an envelope. Opening it, he shook out on to its flap some flakes of a browny-black resinous substance and laid the envelope on the table.

Radley and I examined the dark flakes, while Holmes continued.

'When the boat train left Temple Combe on 30th June it was driven, as we know, by a sober, healthy, experienced crew. Yet before it reached Salisbury something happened to the two men on the footplate that made them behave as if they were asleep. They either failed to see that they were coming into Salisbury, or failed to react properly to that knowledge. Yet they cannot both have fallen asleep and, in fact, we know that at least one of them was aware, in the last seconds before the collision, of their dreadful predicament.'

'How do we know that, Holmes?' I enquired.

'The whistle, Watson! Either Robbins or Gadd held down the whistle handle as they rushed into Salisbury – a last attempt to warn those ahead. In other words, they were overwhelmed by something, between Temple Combe and Salisbury, that made them unaware of what was happening, until one or another realised that disaster was inevitable and sent that last warning.'

'Then I was right – they were drugged!' I exclaimed, looking at the flakes in front of me and remembering my own experiences of the previous night.

'Well done, Watson! Yes, Driver Robbins and Fireman Gadd were made senseless by a powerful opiate.'

'How can it have been administered?' asked Radley. 'Surely, if it were in their food or drink, it cannot have been timed so precisely?'

'It was not in their food or drink, but it did not need to be timed precisely. The maniac's intention was that the Plymouth boat train should not reach London on that night. He knew, as must be evident to you, that a high-speed train, in the control of engine-men who are, to all intents and purposes asleep, will inevitably come to grief somewhere upon its journey.'

'Then how was it administered?' I asked.

'I scraped these flakes', said Holmes, 'from the firebox surround of Number 421 last night. It seems that, while she stood in Temple Combe on 30th June, someone applied to her firebox door a crude form of paint, liberally dosed with what was almost certainly a resinous opiate. As the engine gathered speed from Temple Combe the fumes of that mixture would have been sucked up and out from the firebox by the draught outside the cab, right into the faces of Robbins and Gadd occupying their seats on each side. So, as our crew last night did, they fell into the soporific stupor that the drug induces, leaving their powerful charge to roar on through the night until it found its own doom.'

'Hideous!' said Radley. 'But how did the effect repeat itself last night?'

'Because a deposit of the resin was still on and around Number 421's firebox and because our slow pace reduced the outside draught, causing the weaker fumes of the drug to concentrate more readily in the cab. Neither Watson nor I, with our heads outside, was affected until we turned into the cab. Then Watson breathed in more of the tainted smoke than I simply because I had wrapped my scarf around my mouth as a protection against the wind. As I said last night, gentlemen, we nearly had another tragedy because I broke my own rule and theorised in advance of my data, maintaining that crime was not a possible explanation.'

'Who would commit such a crime, Holmes, and why?' I wondered.

'To discover who, I suggest Mr Radley asks the local police to check with our erstwhile landlady at Temple Combe the date on which a gentleman astronomer called on her. If, as I believe it well may have been, it was the evening of 30th June, I suggest that the most particular description of the astronomer is obtained and circulated. As to why, the short answer is that this maniac's slaughter was simply a convenient device for delaying the Plymouth Express. Once Dr Watson has rested and recovered a little he and I will go to London to talk to someone who can, if he will, give us a longer answer.'

8

A LONGER ANSWER

My own house in Kensington had been shut up in expectation of my holiday at Fulworth, and my modest household sent on their own holidays, so Holmes and I made our London headquarters at an hotel close to Waterloo Station. From there, on the evening after our arrival, we took a cab to Pall Mall and the Diogenes Club.

I have described elsewhere that most extraordinary of London clubs, distinguished by its inflexible rule that members may not speak to one another on the premises. My friend's elder brother, Mycroft Holmes, had been among the club's founders and was now to be found there every evening, enjoying the immunity that he and his colleagues had created. Of Mycroft himself I had seen very little and knew only what Holmes had told me – that he was a superior functionary of the Government; indeed, Holmes claimed that his authority and jurisdiction were so wide that on occasion his brother *was*, to all intents and purposes, the Government. Despite this, I never once recall seeing his name in the newspapers. That so powerful a man was unknown to the public bespeaks not only that discretion with which affairs of state are handled in this country but also his own *modus vivendi*. He lived in chambers on Pall Mall, a stone's throw from his beloved club, and worked at a desk in St James's, little further away. Between those three points he moved with the regularity of a planet in its course, and only the gravest crises could divert him from that orbit. Holmes asserted that Mycroft was his intellectual superior, but that his proscribed existence was dictated by laziness.

The commissionaire of the Diogenes Club showed us into the Strangers' Room, the only room on the premises where conversation was permitted, and we stood, looking out upon Pall Mall and waiting until the door opened and the tall but corpulent figure of Mycroft entered. Despite his build, his features managed to retain some of the sharpness of his younger brother's, but his eyes were a pale, watery grey, entirely without the depth and intensity of my friend's.

'Good-day, Sherlock – and Dr Watson. Is this purely a social visit or does the appearance of both together indicate that you are, as it were, back in harness?'

'Spare us your jests, brother,' said Holmes as we both shook Mycroft's hand. 'You know perfectly well what brings us here.'

'I would guess', said Mycroft, taking a tortoiseshell snuffbox from his pocket, 'that, after first refusing, you succumbed to my friend Borrowclere's pleading and agreed to investigate this business of the night expresses which so bothers him and his fellow directors. Am I right?'

'Of course,' said Holmes.

'And have you had any success in explaining his little mystery?' asked Mycroft as he plied himself with snuff.

'If you mean can I tell you how the Plymouth boat train was derailed and why, then I have had some success. However, as to the identity of the criminal and the precise reasons for his act I have little idea. It is on those points that I have come to consult you.'

'Consult me?' expostulated Mycroft, from behind a large red handkerchief. 'Why do you believe that I have any help to offer?'

'You do us both less than justice by sparring with me,' said Holmes. 'We are too much alike in our mental processes to go far along that road. It was you who sent Borrowclere and his colleagues to me. Furthermore, in the knowledge that I would not willingly involve myself, you armed Borrowclere with your own note, carefully devised, I may add, to mean nothing to Borrowclere while clearly conveying to me the interest of your office in this affair. Is that not so?'

'Really, Sherlock,' said Mycroft, tucking away both snuffbox and handkerchief, 'regrettable as railway accidents are, they are not the province of my office. I would imagine that the Board of Trade or perhaps the Post Office are more likely to be concerned.'

Holmes picked up his hat and turned towards the door. 'Then you will have no objection if I tell the South-Western Railway that it can publish my discoveries relating to the Plymouth Express?'

Mycroft stepped in front of him. 'Do not be so hasty, brother! If you and Dr Watson will take a seat I will see whether I can help your enquiries in any way, but first tell me what you have discovered.'

We seated ourselves and Holmes outlined his conclusions on the derailment. He did not mention the two missing passengers. Mycroft heard his brother's account in silence and remained silent for some moments after it had ended.

'So you are satisfied that the train was deliberately derailed and you have an indication as to the perpetrator. How then can I help you?' he asked at last.

'Firstly by revealing to me the interest that you and His Majesty's Government have in this matter?'

'I am not sure that I am able to do that,' Mycroft replied thoughtfully. 'You must appreciate that I am, on occasions, the repository of secrets that are not my own.'

'Indeed,' said Holmes. 'But in the past you have been ready to trust Watson and me with your own and others' secrets. What secret is involved here that you cannot now trust us?'

Mycroft placed the fingers of his two hands together in front of his face and gazed across them. After a pause, he said, 'This matter impinges upon the most delicate of international negotiations – matters so sensitive that they are known only to a few individuals. That is because their importance is beyond measure. It is no exaggeration to say that they involve the peace of Europe, if not of the whole world.'

Holmes was about to speak, but Mycroft lifted a hand. 'That is not, in itself, a reason why I am reluctant to reveal them to you two. I have never had the least fear for your discretion, but I do fear for your safety. You have discovered for yourself how casually our enemies will murder dozens. How much more casually will they murder two individuals who hinder them? Worse still, what measures will they apply to you if they have any reason to believe that you know anything that might be of use to them?'

'Come now, Mycroft, you know me well enough to know that

once embarked upon an enquiry I will always pursue it to its conclusion, and that danger, while I do not court it, has never discouraged me from an investigation. If you will not reveal the negotiations of which you spoke, at least let me know the identity of our enemy.'

Mycroft laughed. 'The name of the maniac who destroyed the Plymouth train is not known to me, but I have little doubt as to his employers. They operate not far from here – in Carlton House Terrace, to be precise.'

I could not conceal my surprise. 'The German Embassy? But surely . . .!'

'Precisely, Dr Watson. I have now no doubt that the Plymouth Express was derailed on the orders of the Intelligence Service of His Imperial Majesty Kaiser Wilhelm II, or, as his loyal subjects know him, the All Highest.'

'But we are not at war, nor threatening war with Germany!' I expostulated.

'If we are at peace with Germany,' replied Mycroft Holmes, 'it is because we maintain that peace, by a delicate series of manoeuvres that make it impossible for the Kaiser to begin a war.'

'Surely', I argued, 'he is King Edward's nephew, his mother was of British royal blood!'

'True, doctor, true, and while his grandmother was alive he posed no threat. Perhaps if his mother had not died so soon after the Queen he might still have been no problem. However, he has been building battleships with great enthusiasm for the last few years. He resents the power of our Empire and the size of our fleet. Was it not Raleigh who said, "Whosoever commands the sea commands the trade; whosoever commands the trade of the world commands the riches of the world . . ."?'

'". . . and consequently the world itself,"' finished Holmes. 'But surely his ambitions are not so large?'

'He is a strange mixture,' said Mycroft. 'He tells King Edward how proud he is to share the blood of our Royal Family, but at home he rails against the King and accuses him of plotting to encircle and destroy Germany. He wants a fleet to outmatch ours, an Empire greater than ours and markets bigger than ours. With his generals he endlessly plots for what they call *"Der Tag"* – The Day – the day when Germany will strike for all that it wants, all that it believes is its right.'

'Does not our alliance with the French mean that his dreams are impossible?' I asked.

'Until two years ago, the Kaiser believed that the long-standing hostility between Britain and France was such that, if he attacked France or her Russian ally, Britain would not intervene. That is precisely why the King worked so hard to bring about the *Entente Cordiale*. That alliance has enraged His Imperial Majesty. He has challenged the French once at Tangier last year and brought us close to war. The negotiations to which I referred are an attempt to achieve a series of alliances which will make even the All Highest realise that his ambitions cannot be fulfilled and that to attempt a European war will result in the destruction of Germany.'

'An alliance between ourselves and Russia, unlikely as that may be, seems to be the next logical step for us,' said Holmes, 'but your emissary was travelling from the United States, not Russia.'

'My emissary!' exclaimed Mycroft. 'Really, my dear brother, I have underestimated you! What do you know of an emissary?'

Holmes smiled thinly. 'Because you suspected the hand of German Intelligence in the Plymouth boat train affair, you used Borrowclere and Jesson to involve me, apparently so that I might confirm your theory and save you and your office from becoming overtly involved. The Plymouth boat train, as you well know, was attacked because it was believed to be carrying an emissary from the United States who was hurrying to meet you. It is unlikely that an alliance with the Czar would be negotiated on the far side of the Atlantic. Are you, by any chance, seeking to secure the peace of Europe by persuading our American cousins to discard their historic attitude of non-involvement in European affairs?'

Mycroft's watery eyes rested on his brother for a long time before he responded. 'I see you have thought your way further into this affair than I believed, Sherlock. I do not know how you have divined the presence of my emissary on that train, but that knowledge must remain most secret. Its publication would endanger His Majesty's efforts and its possession endangers

49

the possessors. Have you communicated your discoveries to anyone?'

'Radley of the South-Western Railway has been told how his train was destroyed, but not the reason, and I have laid an embargo on his revealing anything, even to his fellow directors, unless I permit it.'

'Good! That is excellent, but for your own sakes I recommend that you now leave the matter with me. These are extremely dangerous affairs.'

'I have crossed swords with the agents of the All Highest before, Mycroft.'

'So you have, Sherlock, but this time we are not dealing with small fry like Oberstein, who pick up trifles. Here we are pitted against their best and deadliest agents who are meddling with the very mechanisms which maintain the peace of the world.'

'You forget, Mycroft, that I am retained by your friends in the railway companies to investigate their tragedies for them and that, so far, the job is incomplete, to say nothing of the fact that the most homicidal lunatic in Britain remains unpunished. Whether you will assist us or not, Watson and I will go on to examine the Edinburgh mail train incident.'

'Since you know how it was done at Salisbury, it is surely superfluous to investigate at Grantham?' said Mycroft.

'Unless you can assure me', said Holmes, rising to his feet, 'that there was no reason for German Intelligence to interfere with the Edinburgh train, then it must be investigated.'

There was a long silence, during which Holmes stared steadfastly at his brother. At last it was he who broke the silence.

'Come, Watson,' he said. 'It appears that this particular barrel has been scraped.'

Mycroft sprang to his feet, faster than I had ever seen him move before. 'The telegram!' he exclaimed. 'That's how you discovered my emissary!'

Holmes laughed. 'Your sedentary life dulls you, brother. Yes, it was the telegram, and speaking of telegrams you might do me a favour if you will.'

'If I can,' said Mycroft.

'If your office has any influence over the Postmaster-General, I should very much like to know the details of a telegram sent on the afternoon or evening of 30th June – most probably from Plymouth – to the village post office at Temple Combe for delivery to a guest at the village inn there. Knowing the sanctity of the Post Office and the honesty of public servants I have forborne to embarrass the postmaster there by questioning him.'

THE VANISHING GENTLEMEN

Holmes and I remained at our hotel the next day, where Holmes prepared himself for our enquiries at Grantham as thoroughly as he had before we went to Temple Combe. Borrowclere had supplied his company's documents on the Grantham catastrophe, together with large-scale maps of the line and the stations, and Holmes studied them assiduously.

In mid-morning two telegrams arrived for Holmes, and he laughed before passing them to me. The first was from Greenwich Observatory and read:

NO SIGNIFICANT LUNAR OR ASTRONOMICAL PHENOMENA VISIBLE ON SOMERSET WILTS BORDER JUNE 30 JULY 1 STOP MAY WE KNOW REASON FOR YOUR ENQUIRY STOP

The second was from Mycroft and ran:

POSTMASTER TEMPLE COMBE CONFIRMS RECEIPT OF MESSAGE FROM PLYMOUTH 30 JUNE FOR MILLER REPEAT MILLER AT TEMPLE COMBE AS FOLLOWS MOON PASSES BY LINE NOT COAST STOP ARRANGE FOR ECLIPSE YOUR AREA STOP SIGNATURE Z REPEAT Z STOP HOPE THIS ASSISTS – M

'So our experimental astronomer in Somerset was a fraud,' said Holmes when I had read them both.

'As you guessed, Holmes,' I remarked.

'As I surmised, Watson,' he corrected me. 'It is permissible to theorise in directions that do not contradict the facts as we know them, but it is unwise to go very far in that direction without checking the facts. My knowledge of astronomy, as you have publicly remarked, is limited, but I think we may take the word of the experts at Greenwich. Unfortunately I fear we shall have to leave them in ignorance of the reasons for our enquiry, not only because of my dear brother but because they would probably not believe our explanation.'

'And the second telegram?' I asked.

'Merely confirms the first. The so-called astronomer was evidently the German agent placed in Temple Combe until a confederate at Plymouth confirmed whether Mycroft's emissary travelled by sea or rail from Plymouth. Having received his message, couched in terms sufficiently scientific to mislead telegraph operators, it was then his task to stop the Plymouth train reaching London that night. Now we must wait and see what information comes from Temple Combe before we depart for Peterborough.'

Midday brought Radley, hotfoot from Waterloo Station, and over lunch he outlined the results of the enquiries at Temple Combe.

'It seems', he told us, 'that the astronomer, who went by the name of Miller, incidentally, arrived from London in the middle of the day. A porter remembers assisting a gentleman with some unusually shaped luggage, including a long, tubular, leather case, at about that time. He believes the passenger came off a down train.'

'Is there any way of checking?' asked Holmes.

'I have myself examined the tickets taken from passengers alighting at Temple Combe that day. There are only three from Waterloo. Before coming here I checked the serial numbers at Waterloo. Two would have been issued in time for the holders to be in Temple Combe at lunch-time. What is more, the ticket collector in Somerset also recollects a person with unusual luggage coming off a London train and recalls him enquiring about an inn.'

'Splendid!' cried Holmes. 'Radley, I could not have done better myself! So, in addition to mine host and his lady, your porter and ticket collector have seen this man. Can they describe him? What was he like?'

'There's the rub, Mr Holmes,' said Radley. 'They all describe the same man, but I doubt if their descriptions will take us far. They all agree that he was of moderate height and build, well-dressed for the country in a light suit with a wide-brimmed straw hat. They cannot agree as to the colour of his eyes, but are all agreed that his hair was of a medium fairness and he wore a full set of whiskers.'

'Which may, of course, have been false,' said Holmes, 'leaving us with a person of medium colouring and average height and build. Not much of a help! How did he speak? Was there any trace of an accent?'

'I'm afraid not, Mr Holmes. They all say that he spoke "like a gentleman" and if there had been any accent I'm sure they'd have noticed. Country people are quick to notice anything like that.'

When Radley had gone, and we could talk freely, I reopened the subject.

'If this so-called astronomer was the maniac who derailed the Plymouth Express it is astonishing that he has no accent, Holmes!'

'Why so, Watson? Why so? It is only in Sexton Blake stories that all foreign spies have obvious accents.'

'Holmes, I have learned that there are citizens of this country whose loyalties can be bought or perverted to the service of another nation, but no Briton could have committed that crime!'

My friend laughed. 'Good old Watson!' he exclaimed. 'When we succeed in returning to Fulworth, read my commonplace books. There you will find the records of the most hideous crimes committed by ordinary British men and women. Mary Arnold, the Female Monster, who blinded her child with live beetles placed under walnut shells and bound over its eyes; Palmer, a country practitioner of your own profession, who shared your fondness for the turf and supported his interest by poisoning his friends; Mrs Cotten, the Yorkshire murderess; the dreadful Burke and Hare with their associate Knox, another gentleman of your profession, Watson. The list is endless, old friend, in this country as in others. No crime can be distinguished as belonging entirely to a particular nation.'

'I still find it difficult to believe that he is British,' I replied.

'We shall see, Watson, we shall see. At present we know only that he is virtually indistinguishable in a crowd and practises astronomy.'

'Then you believe he is, in fact, an astronomer?' I exclaimed.

'I should be very surprised if he were not,' said Holmes, 'for an astronomical telescope is a strange property with which to support a false character unless you happen to have one by you. Now, let us make our way to King's Cross and see what traces of Mr Miller we may find in Peterborough.'

We left that afternoon for Peterborough, where Holmes commenced his investigations almost as soon as we arrived at our hotel. Accosting the manager, he adopted a discursive, academic manner to explain his enquiries.

'I had been hoping to hear from my friend Mr Miller. Like me he is an enthusiastic astronomer – he came here, you know, with his equipment, to observe a transit of Venus. I was so looking forward to his account of the phenomenon – I don't have the leisure, you see – but he has sent not a word. Now it occurs to me that he was going on to Scotland. I wondered if he was somehow involved in that dreadful railway episode – no word from him since, you see.'

The manager was a model of patience, but eventually succeeded in interrupting my friend's flow. 'I'm sure that nothing has happened to your friend, sir, but how do you believe I can help you?'

'I wondered if, by any chance, he had stayed at this hotel? If he was still here after the rail disaster I would know he was not involved. It is so unlike him not to correspond!'

To stem this flood the manager was only too willing to try and recollect 'Mr Miller' and his telescope, but without success. Nor was his register of any help, but he did provide us with the names of the most likely places at which to continue our enquiries. The remainder of the evening passed in visiting each one of them, where Holmes would repeat his performance. We had visited four, and were growing discouraged, when our persistence bore fruit. The landlady of a quiet commercial hotel remembered our astronomer and was able to assure us that he had not come to grief. He had gone out in the evening, with his equipment for an experiment, and returned late. Rising late the next morning, he had expressed himself satisfied with the experiment and departed back to London after breakfast.

There, to corroborate her, was his name in the register on 19th September – 'Francis Miller, 19a Upper Scardale Street, London.'

My friend thanked the good lady profusely and we were soon back at our hotel. Before we retired for the night I asked him, 'Now you have confirmed the presence of the astronomer, there is surely no need to enquire further?'

'You think not, Watson?' he replied. 'Have you forgotten my brother's silence when he tried to persuade me to abandon this investigation and I asked for his assurance that German Intelligence had no reason to tamper with the Edinburgh Mail? No, Watson, our enquiries are not completed. We still have no idea why our astronomical maniac attacked the Edinburgh train.'

The next morning we spent at Peterborough Station, talking to those who were working there on the fatal night. Once again, the witnesses only served to confirm the information given us by the Great Northern Railway directors. We had gained no new information when Holmes asked a porter:

'Did you have any occasion to take any particular note of any of the passengers while the train was here?'

'Only one gentleman, sir. There was a tall gentleman in the first class. He got down while the train was here and I seen him walking the platform, stretching his legs, I expect.'

'Could you describe him more exactly?' asked Holmes keenly.

'Well, sir, he was as tall as you, or maybe a shade more, but much bigger in the body than you, sir. Corpulent, you might say. As I was coming down here he stepped down from the first class and was walking up and down. When I came back he was still walking up and down. He was looking at his watch, checking she was on time, I suppose. I didn't see him again for I was down by the mail coach until she went out.'

'That must have been him as met the motor-car gentleman!' interjected a boy who stood near us.

'The motor-car gentleman!' repeated Holmes. 'Who was that?'

'Please sir, I'm a telegraph boy, sir, and I was at the telegraph office when I heard a motor coming in the front, so I ran out to look. A big Mercedes came right up to the entrance, sir. He was going like the wind, sir, and I didn't think he'd stop in time!'

'Did you see who was in it?' asked Holmes.

'Oh yes, sir. There was the driver, sir, but he was all in his goggles and cap so I never got a good look at him, but there was a gentleman as he was driving, sir. He was a stout gentleman, sir, and I think he had a bad leg, for he seemed to have difficulty getting down from the car.'

'How was he dressed?'

'He had a travelling cape, sir, and a big wide hat pulled down over his face.'

'Did you see his face?'

'No sir, only as he'd got a beard and he was smoking a cigar. He didn't have no luggage with him and once he was out of the car he just waved his hand to the driver and went straight through the booking hall. When the car was gone I went back on to the platform and I seen that gent and the one the porter was telling you about. The tall gentleman was helping the other into the first class. I didn't see no more, for the Edinburgh went out just as soon as they got on.'

'Excellent!' said Holmes, and gave the youth a coin. 'Now, Watson, we must speak to the ticket collector and confirm that the motor-car gentleman, as our young friend called him, had no ticket for anywhere.'

'But he must have had a ticket for somewhere!' I exclaimed.

'On the contrary, Watson, it is extremely unlikely that that gentleman had a ticket!'

We were unable to resolve the issue. The ticket collector who had been on duty that night was not available to us, and shortly afterwards we left for Grantham.

On the journey to Grantham Holmes was a different man. He hummed snatches of melody and refused to discuss the case with me, discoursing instead on the passing countryside. I knew the mood of old to signify that he had now entered deeply into the complexities of the case and expected a new revelation shortly.

At Grantham Station we met Signalman Day, who took us to the south signal box and showed us how he had seen Driver Fleetwood and Fireman Talbot on the footplate of their doomed locomotive. 'They was one each side,' he told us, 'just a-staring through the spectacle glasses as if they didn't know where in the world they was. And the next thing she was away past and into the station.'

Night Inspector Pile and the postmen who had waited for the train on the platform told us how it had thundered past them; Postman Cox, spying the mail coach on the train, had been the first to realise what had occurred. 'We turned and watched it go through,' he said. 'It went out under the red lights and the next minute there was a great bang, like an explosion, and all flames up there.'

We walked to the scene of the wreck, looking at the under-bridge, where the driverless train had torn away the para-pet, and the embankment where the shattered wreckage had tumbled and burned. Here another dozen souls had been added to the hellish record of the madman with a telescope.

Holmes questioned the railway staff about the two travellers who had been described to us at Peterborough. They had survived the wreck, for a porter recalled that, amidst the carnage and confusion of that fearful night, the station master had called a telegraph boy to take two gentlemen to his office and attend to their needs. The boy's description fitted our two mysterious travellers.

'I never heard the short one speak, sir,' he told us. 'I took them to the station master's room and the tall one asked if I could find them some tea and he wanted ginger biscuits. Well, there was tea, but we didn't have no ginger biscuits, so I asked the station master and he said to knock up Grocer Roberts, as it was important as these gentlemen had what they wanted. So I went to Grocer Roberts. He wasn't best pleased to be got out at that time and he wanted to know who was paying. I told him I was from the Great Northern and there'd been an accident, but he wouldn't let me have the biscuits till I paid for them. He's a mean one he is, sir, always going on about how the Liberals is spoiling the country. So I had to pay for the ginger nuts, sir, but I got them and give them to the two gentlemen, and it was all right, for when they went the tall gentleman give me a whole sovereign for looking after them!'

'And when did they go?' asked Holmes.

'About two hours after the Edinburgh was wrecked they went. There was a special brought down to the other side of the wreck to take them and they went off.'

'Ha!' exclaimed Holmes. 'You did well, my boy,' and he gave

the lad another sovereign. 'Come, Watson. We have, I think, learned all that is useful here!'

On the way to our hotel I questioned my friend as to the mysterious travellers.

'Watson!' he exclaimed. 'You have the data but you do not understand it! Who, in this affair, is as tall as I but corpulent?'

'Why! Your brother Mycroft,' I said. 'But you yourself have said that he never leaves his office, his chambers or his club if he can avoid it! Surely he is not one of the men on the Edinburgh train?'

'Who else?' asked Holmes. 'Something had occurred of such gravity that even my lethargic brother was forced to travel to Scotland in haste, and to meet his master on the way.'

'His master?' I asked.

'Edward VII, by the Grace of God King of England, Emperor of India and Defender of the Faith! The Mercedes and the ginger biscuits confirm my suspicions. Mycroft makes an entirely uncharacteristic and hurried journey to Scotland. Who else commands that degree of devotion from my brother but the King? At Peterborough a mysterious passenger arrives by motor car to join him and, despite the wreck, they continue their journey by a special train. Something was afoot in Scotland that drew them both in haste from London and from Sandringham!'

'Then we are going to Scotland?' I queried.

'You excel yourself, Watson. Yes, we will spend one night in this excessively dull town and tomorrow we shall depart for Scotland.'

'It is a long time since I have seen Edinburgh,' I remarked.

'Nor will you see much of it now,' said Holmes, 'for we are going to Aberdeen.'

10

A CRACK SHOT

The long journey to the North passed pleasantly enough. Holmes was in high good humour, partly, I suspect, at having uncovered facts which Mycroft had concealed from him. Certainly he made occasional sardonic references to his brother and his attempts to persuade us to desist from our investigation, but otherwise he chatted in an animated fashion on the customary wide range of fascinating topics.

In Aberdeen we settled ourselves in a plain but homely hotel not far from the city's great docks. Holmes let it be known to the proprietor that I was a writer from a London magazine and that he was an artist. We had come to the Scottish coast to prepare an illustrated essay on the fishing trade carried on in the area. These characters required a little in the way of costume, and on our first outing in the city I wore one of my less reputable outfits with a soft cap, while Holmes appeared in velveteen jacket and a loose cravat with no hat.

The public buildings of Aberdeen are, in many cases, constructed of granite from the nearby mountains and while in grey weather this can impart a threatening air, in the clear autumnal sunlight of that morning they glowed like pearls, sparkling wherever the morning sun struck the particles of mica in the stone. Holmes' interest, however, was in the seaport itself, and soon we were in more functional streets of towering warehouses, where the traffic consisted of great wagons piled with barrels and carts stacked with slatted boxes of fish and crushed ice.

The strengthening odour of fish as much as the sight of masts and spars above the rooftops confirmed our direction and soon we came out upon a cobbled quayside. Here all was activity, for a number of fishing vessels had brought home their catch. The shouts of seamen unloading their vessels mingled with a strange chanting sound from another part of the quay where fish was being auctioned by a small man standing atop a barrel and calling his bids at a breathless speed and in a jargon that I do not recall hearing before. Further along were sturdy trestle tables, set in the open air, where bevies of young women were hard at work with fearsome knives, gutting fish as if their lives depended on it and flinging them into barrels of brine. Everywhere was the sight and smell of fish, and over it all wheeled clouds of clamorous gulls, adding their cries to the general din and swooping, when opportunity offered, to gulp a titbit from the water or the cobbles.

'Good heavens!' I said to Holmes, as my eyes and ears absorbed the frenzied activity and noise. 'Is this a place where anyone will pause to give us information?'

My companion chuckled. 'At present these good people are concerned with the urgent and very important business of ensuring a proper supply of breakfast kippers,' he replied. 'For the moment we must stroll about in our assumed characters. You will make copious notes and I will effect a few sketches, during which time we shall keep our eyes peeled for foreign vessels of any nationality. Later, when these cargoes have been wholly unloaded, sold and packed, we shall find people who will talk to us.'

The bustle did, eventually, lessen, and by midday we were able to find many of the morning's workers in the quayside taverns, where our English accents attracted as much attention as our costume and a few shillings spent on whisky made us a number of friends. Holmes modestly displayed his sketch-block, which, somewhat to my surprise, contained some very creditable renderings of people and ships. He explained our professional interest in the port and all its visitors, expressing particular wonder at the range of foreign vessels. Native pride set our drinking companions to listing the many ports of Northern Europe whose ships visited Aberdeen, and I dutifully scribbled notes.

When the conversation lapsed, Holmes enquired innocently, 'Do you see any Russian vessels in Aberdeen?'

'They used to come here noo and then,' said one bearded

fisherman, 'trawlers, timber ships, all sorts, but since yon affair wi' the Hull trawlers they've been a wee bit shy of oor fishing ports!'

His colleagues growled and nodded assent around the table, and I realised they were referring to the incident some two years previously, when the Czar's fleet passing through the North Sea on its way to Japan had shelled a group of English fishing boats in the belief that they were Japanese.

For the rest of the day we continued our exploration of the port, noting ships of almost every nationality in Northern Europe apart from Russian. In the evening, at our hotel, Holmes read through my lists of the names of vessels and their ports of origin and then flung the notebook down with an exclamation of impatience.

'Watson,' he said, 'I remain convinced that there has been a Russian ship here recently, and it might still be here, yet no one has seen one. Surely I have not misled myself!'

Day after day we repeated our perambulation of the quays with sketch-block and notebook, sampling all of the dockside inns and talking to seamen and fish girls, dockers and fish porters, but nowhere did we find a hint of the presence of a Russian ship. We saw the many different vessels that came and went from Aberdeen, from the trawlers, some of which seemed hardly bigger than a Thames launch, to graceful Scandinavian clippers, and from dirty steam colliers up from the Tyne to the big, red-sailed barges from the Thames.

We had been nearly a week in the city when we stood one day admiring a tall four-masted clipper whose stern proclaimed her out of Esbjerg on the Jutland peninsula. Holmes took out pad and pencil and commenced a sketch. After a few moments a tall, lean man, with a Viking's hair and beard, unseated himself from a bollard by her forward gangway and strolled across to watch. As Holmes completed his drawing and put the sketch-block under his arm, the man stepped up and took his empty pipe from his mouth.

'Excuse, gentlemen,' he said, in the unmistakably liquid accent of Scandinavia. 'You were making a picture of our ship, ya? May I please see it?'

'By all means,' replied Holmes affably, and opened his pad again, showing a strong, clearly limned sketch of the vessel.

'You draw good, ya!' said the seaman. 'But you should draw her when she is sailing, so land people can see how she looks in stiff weather.'

'Have you been long in harbour?' I asked.

'Only since this morning,' he replied. 'We are here empty for cargo. Day before yesterday we discharge at Stonehaven.'

'And are you returning to Russia?' asked Holmes innocently.

'To Russia? No, no, gentlemen. We are from Esbjerg in Danmark. You think we are Russian, ya?' and he laughed loudly.

'I beg your pardon,' said Holmes, taking out his tobacco pouch and offering our acquaintance a fill. 'I understood that Russian ships come into Aberdeen and I thought your accent was Russian.'

'No, my friends,' said the sailor. 'I am good Dansker, like your Queen, ya? And the Russian ships, they do not come so much after they shoot at your trawlers. But today we see one.'

'Really?' said Holmes. 'In the harbour here?'

'Not here,' said our friend, drawing on his pipe. 'This morning, yust before the sun is up, we are south, coming from Stonehaven, standing well out to catch the breeze, ya? We see Russian boat, very fancy, running into little port south from here.'

'Do you remember which port it was entering?' asked Holmes.

'Little place down coast,' said the Dane. 'I cannot tell name, but there was fancy steam yacht with Russian flag. You want to draw her, ya?'

'I would very much like to draw her!' said Holmes, and thanked our informant warmly, finally presenting him with the sketch of his ship.

We strolled away, but as soon as we were out of sight of the sailor Holmes swung round to me with his eyes blazing.

'A Russian yacht entering a port to the south of here – and only yesterday at dawn!' he exclaimed. 'There is not a moment to lose! We need a good map and a carriage!'

Hurrying back to our lodgings we equipped ourselves with maps and had food packed while a carriage was hired. In less than an hour we were trotting out of Aberdeen on the southern coast road.

Our rail journey had revealed and the map confirmed that the fifteen miles or so of coast that lie between Aberdeen and Stonehaven are dotted at short intervals with small seaside villages. Still in our guise of writer and artist we now visited each in turn. They were all much alike, small collections of stone cottages, huddled on the cliff top or gathered around a harbour cluttered with little fishing boats and their apparatus, some facing out to the North Sea, others with more sheltered havens. As we journeyed from one to another I asked Holmes the significance of the Russian yacht.

'There lies the duplicity of my diplomatic brother!' he exclaimed. 'Mycroft was unwilling to reveal the existence of his American negotiations until I forced his hand. He did not wish us to look closely into the Grantham affair, despite the peril in which the King himself had been placed. In other words, some other secret lay behind Mycroft's journey to Scotland with the King. It is the most natural thing for King Edward to travel from his estate at Sandringham to his Scottish home, but the most unusual for him to be accompanied by my brother. They travelled to meet another emissary, Watson, this time an emissary of the Czar, slipping quietly into Scotland across the North Sea!'

'Are you proposing to intervene in these negotiations?' I asked, somewhat alarmed.

'No, Watson. International alliances are Mycroft's business. Mine is a commission to explain the railway crashes and a determination to bring to justice the monstrous lunatic who has murdered forty people for political ends. I had thought when we came north that I could establish my belief in the Russian negotiation and use it to extract further information from my brother. I sought merely to prove that a Russian emissary had been in Scotland when the Edinburgh Mail was derailed. Fate has dealt kindly with us and sent the messenger back, and you may be sure that where Mycroft's messenger is, the agents of the All Highest will be only a step behind!'

Late in the afternoon we found our quarry. At the quayside of a tiny fishing village lay a gleaming steam yacht, a thoroughbred among the mongrel fishing boats that were moored about it. Conversation with the locals revealed that this stranger had put in on the previous morning, claiming a difficulty with her engines. Little had been seen of her crew, save a youth who had taken telegrams to the post office.

Armed again with notebook and sketch-pad we strolled on to the jetty where she lay. A squat, dark-bearded sailor stood on her deck, leaning with his arms on the rail near her bow. He took no notice of our arrival, but when Holmes opened his pad and began to draw the sailor went below, to return in a moment with a youth in seaman's cap, jersey and boots. They conversed together rapidly in low tones, then the boy stepped to the top of the gangplank, his right hand held behind his back.

'You gentlemen!' he called in our direction. 'This is private ship. It is not to be drawn! Please to go away! You must not make pictures of it!'

'But she is a very handsome vessel!' replied Holmes. 'My friend and I were just admiring her. Surely there is no harm in me making a drawing of her?'

'It is private ship! It is not to be drawn!' repeated the boy, stepping on to the gangplank. 'If you will not go, I must make you!' and he drew his right hand from behind his back, revealing that he held a large revolver.

'Very well,' said Holmes evenly. 'We are sorry to cause you any concern,' and he closed his pad and turned away. Together we crossed the quayside towards the village inn.

The pistol shot took us completely by surprise. It snatched Holmes' pad from beneath his arm and scattered its leaves across the quay. Whirling, I saw the boy and the sailor disappearing below decks.

'Holmes!' I cried. 'Are you hurt?'

'Oh no, Watson,' he replied. 'It was far too good a shot for that!'

He stooped and began to gather the remnants of his sketches, a thoughtful look in his eye. 'What a curious way of speaking that young man has!' he said.

11

AN AMBUSH ON THE MOORS

It required a glass of good Highland whisky at the inn to restore my calm, but Holmes seemed hardly to have been ruffled by our experience on the quay. He arranged lodgings for us both, in a room overlooking the jetty, and, after dinner, asked me to take our carriage back to Aberdeen.

'Be so good', he asked me, 'as to tell the hotel in Aberdeen our commission is completed and we are returning to London. Before you return in the morning there are one or two other things you may do. I had not expected to come close to our quarry so soon and I fear we may be ill prepared. There are huntsmen's shops, I feel certain, in Aberdeen, and it should be possible to obtain a pair of good field-glasses. In addition, I have no weapon and I doubt if you have your old bulldog with you.'

I admitted that, in setting out for a fortnight's holiday on the Sussex coast, I had not packed my revolver.

'Then I suggest that you add to the shopping list a pair of serviceable pistols and two boxes of smokeless ammunition. We would, I think, be foolish to ignore entirely my brother's assessment of the opposition.'

I returned to the village late on the following morning and found Holmes at the inn, listening with every sign of enjoyment to the garrulous reminiscences of an elderly fisherman whom he was plying with whisky. He greeted me cheerfully as I entered the bar, and introduced his companion.

'This is Mr Mackenzie, who has been telling me of his quite remarkable life at sea. I have explained to him that you and I are preparing a magazine article upon the fishing trade, and I am sure he will give you plenty of material. Do you know, he tells me that the handsome yacht across the quay is from Russia?'

'Really?' I said, with as much surprise as I felt able to muster, but the aged seaman soon explained Holmes' interest in him.

'Oh aye,' he said. 'It's frae Roossia allright. Ma sister keeps the post office and since they came in they've done naething but send telegrams aboot their engines. They've been sending tae Aiberdeen and two tae the Russian Embassy in London. It seems they want some new-fangled piece for their machinery that they cannae get hereaboots, so they're having one made in Aiberdeen!'

Mr Mackenzie passed the afternoon with us in an endless flood of reminiscence, while I took occasional notes and my friend's eyes hardly left the window as he watched the quayside.

After dark we dined and took ourselves off at an early hour to our room. Once inside the somewhat spartan bedroom, Holmes doused the candles and we sat by the window, observing the harbour. The Russian yacht lay silent at the jetty, with no sign of life other than a single sailor smoking a pipe on her foredeck. At around midnight Holmes deemed it safe for us to take to our beds.

For three days we adopted an unvarying routine. We would consume a hearty Scots breakfast then take ourselves off to the hills inland from the village. There Holmes established a vantage point, well screened by scrub and heather, from which we could watch the harbour without ourselves being obvious. From this concealment we took turns in spying on our quarry all day, aided by the field-glasses which I had brought from Aberdeen.

Each evening we returned to the inn, where Holmes would ply the loquacious Mackenzie with whisky and sort small grains of information from the old man's quantities of chaff. It was this process that eventually produced results. Tapping a finger to his great, bony nose, Mackenzie leaned low across the table one evening and imparted the latest gossip gleaned improperly from his sister's office.

'Yon Roossians'll be awa' soon,' he said.

'Really?' said Holmes. 'I thought they were still in difficulties with an engine part?'

'Oh aye,' said our companion. 'But that's a' fixed the noo'. There's twa sailors and the boy gannin' tae Aiberdeen the morra' tae see tae it.'

'Mr Mackenzie,' said Holmes admiringly, 'is there anything at all that takes place in this vicinity that you do not know?'

The flattery had the desired effect of producing more information.

'They'd a telegram frae Aiberdeen the day. I mind the verra' words. It said, "if test successful you may sail in foorty-eight hoors" – those are the verra' words o' it!'

'Wonderful!' said Holmes, and changed the subject.

Later, in our little bedroom, Holmes' eyes blazed with excitement and he rubbed his hands with pleasure.

'So the Russians are on the move,' he said, 'and not to Aberdeen, I'll be bound! Watson, this should draw the Kaiser's men from hiding! Make sure that both our pistols are loaded!'

He woke me before dawn, lighting a candle and hissing my name. 'Come,' he said, when I was fully awake. 'We must be away before they can see us!'

We dressed in haste, pocketed our revolvers, and left the inn by the back stairs, Holmes leaving some coins on the parlour table and a note explaining to our hostess that some journalistic emergency had called us to Stonehaven by the early train.

'If they are going to Aberdeen, Holmes, why are we going to Stonehaven?' I enquired, as we strode rapidly along the road towards the railway station in the next village.

'Firstly, as I remarked last night, I very much doubt that Aberdeen is their destination, and secondly, we are going no further than the railway station at present, where we shall see what use may be made of those handsomely printed pasteboards with which the London and South-Western have supplied us.'

At the tiny railway station the production of our *laissez-passers* more than supported Holmes' story that we were agents of the company concerned about the safety of goods in transit. They gained for us not only the comfort of the station master's little parlour while we waited for the first Aberdeen train, but the loan of two porters' coats and caps when Holmes requested them.

As the time of the train drew near, a small crowd began

to gather on the Aberdeen platform, most of them third-class passengers drawn from among the working people of the area, but eventually our trio materialised – the yacht's boy, the stocky seaman we had seen on the first day and a tall, good-looking man who was also in seaman's garb but whose features were covered by a close beard. They peered suspiciously at their fellow travellers and drew apart, muttering among themselves.

When the train drew in the trio boarded quickly, jumping into a third-class compartment and slamming the door to behind them. Holmes and I had placed our overcoats and hats in a wicker hamper, and now, clad in our porters' disguise, we humped the basket into the guard's van of the train, where Holmes again produced our spurious credentials to the astonished guard. A mournful note from the whistle and three heavy blasts from the engine signalled our departure, and soon we were *en route* for Aberdeen.

At each of the little stations that interrupted our journey, Holmes would don the porter's cap again and watch from the window to see that the Russian party did not leave the train. At Aberdeen the station was busy with workers and goods, and sufficiently crowded for us to loiter a little way behind our quarry without them spotting us, but they did not leave the station, merely changing platforms and boarding a local train that was already waiting.

'Just as I thought, Watson!' chortled Holmes, as we slipped into a first-class compartment of the same train. 'Their destination was not Aberdeen!'

Soon the train pulled out and, once we had passed the limits of the city, I realised that we were travelling along the left bank of the River Dee, which rises in the Cairngorm Mountains, some sixty miles west of Aberdeen, and flows almost due east across Scotland to the North Sea. The further westward we progressed, the merrier became my companion's mood, as he seemed to see some unspoken prediction justified.

The porter's cap had accompanied us, and on this journey I kept watch under its peak at each station. At Ballater our vigilance was rewarded, for our party left the train. As soon as they had left the platform, Holmes and I sprang from the train. We approached the ticket collector's gate with caution, but we need not have worried for, by the time we left the little station, the Russians were out of sight.

'Where have they gone, Holmes?' I asked, looking in both directions.

'There is now no doubt at all of that!' he replied. 'And you and I have a brisk walk in front of us, so let us acquire some refreshments.'

We crammed our pockets with eatables at the village shop, after which Holmes set out with a determined stride to the west of the village. Once we were beyond immediate observation from the village, he abandoned the road entirely and struck a course into the hills to the south-west. Following him across the heather I tried to reconstruct in my mind's eye the map of this part of Scotland, only to recall that the area we were entering consisted entirely of high and desolate moorland, threaded by a myriad small streams and rising to the occasional peak.

We were now well into October, and sufficiently far north for the air to be distinctly colder than in London, despite the brightness of the day. Nevertheless I was perspiring freely when Holmes eventually called a halt for refreshment. Having been deprived of any breakfast and with an appetite sharpened by our recent exercise, I fell to with a will, as we sat in the heather. Holmes, though, ate sparingly, and held the field-glasses in his right hand, scanning a distant valley running through which I could just discern the white thread of a road.

After a few minutes of this observation he cried, 'Aha! Just as I thought!' and passed me the glasses. Looking in the direction he indicated, with the help of the powerful lenses I saw our three sailors striding along the distant road. 'Well, Watson,' said Holmes, 'what do you make of that?'

'Only that they are a long way from the sea and apparently not about the business of collecting an engine part,' I said, returning the glasses.

'No, indeed,' said Holmes. 'They are, in fact, about to pay a visit to an expert in mechanisms far more delicate and unreliable than the machinery of their yacht. Look!' He pointed, and passed me the field-glasses again. 'They are leaving the road!'

Sure enough, they had turned aside and, like us, taken to the moorland. Holmes sprang to his feet, glanced at the sun, and set off again through the heather, making a more northerly line along the shoulder of a ridge to our left. The sun was south of us, behind the ridge, which gave us the advantage of being hidden in its shadow, whereas the moor across which the sailors were moving west was in open sunlight, and we were able to watch their movements with ease.

Our brisk pace along the ridge soon brought us to its westerly end, where it looked down upon the junction of two deep glens, each threaded by a tumbling stream. Across from us the hillside was well covered with birch scrub and a few larger trees which, though browned by frost, were still in leaf. The Russian party was still some distance to the north and east of us, traversing the valley below the ridge.

Holmes paused where a clump of small, windswept birches thrust up amid a tumble of boulders, and crouched behind them with his field-glasses trained on the Russians. I squatted beside him, completely mystified, as he turned the glasses across the junction of the glens below and searched the entire landscape.

'This is the perfect spot!' he muttered. 'They must be here somewhere!'

'Who, Holmes?' I enquired.

'There! Look!' he hissed suddenly, pointing at the wooded slopes across the junction of the glens. 'Did you not catch it, Watson? The sun flashed on glass or metal. There – above that band of rocks!'

I strained my eyes in the direction he indicated, and suddenly I caught it – a tiny but brilliant point of light, where the southerly sun had caught some shining surface under the trees.

'What is it, Holmes?' I asked.

'Field-glasses perhaps, or a telescope,' he said, training his own glasses on the area. 'No, by heaven! A telescopic rifle sight! We have found them, Watson, we have found them!'

'Then the Russians are walking into an ambush!' I said, as the situation revealed itself to me. 'Should we not warn them, Holmes?'

'Not yet, my friend, not yet! They are in no danger until they clear the shoulder of the valley and emerge by the stream. Let us use that time to move further down the slope, before our friends under the trees get a clear shot at their target!'

We crept, as fast and as stealthily as we might, down the

incline, taking advantage of every rock and patch of shade, until Holmes halted me with his hand on my arm. We were then some fifty yards above the valley's bottom, crouched on the shady side of a huge boulder. Below us and to our left the sailors were stepping steadily forward towards the open junction of the valleys.

Holmes scanned the wooded slopes opposite with his glasses. With his left hand he passed me his pistol from his pocket. 'Take both pistols, Watson,' he commanded softly, 'and, when I give the word, put four shots across the top of that band of rocks.'

I braced myself against our rock and lined both pistols on the point where I had seen the flash earlier. Holmes kept the glasses on the rocks opposite, occasionally turning his eyes from the field-glasses to watch the Russians' progress. The afternoon was now warm, but the perspiration was cooling on me at the thought of the unseen enemy who lay hidden in the distant trees and his unsuspecting target below.

'Now, Watson!' hissed Holmes, and I squeezed both triggers twice. Above the explosions of my pistols I caught the flat, high crack of rifles from among the trees and heard the whine of a ricochet among the rocks beneath us.

The tallest of the three sailors had been hit, it seemed, by a rifle shot, but was still on foot, and all three ran for cover in the rocks around the stream. Holmes snatched his pistol back from me and we tumbled down the slope, while a positive fusillade of rifle fire erupted from the far slope, some of it directed at us.

We reached the valley bottom without mishap and began to work our way cautiously towards the Russians. The unseen riflemen were now keeping up a steady fire across the boulders where the Russians lay, bullets constantly singing among the rocks. From our new position we could see the muzzle flashes of their weapons.

'There seem to be four of them, Holmes!' I cried.

'Yes,' he replied, 'and no shortage of ammunition! Let us see if we can join forces with the Russians.'

We continued creeping towards the sailors, until only a space of about sixty yards separated us from them. There was, however, no cover at all in that space and, in the end, we were forced to rise and make a dash for their stronghold while rifle bullets struck splinters from the boulders around.

Reaching their position we tumbled into the semi-circle of rocks that they occupied.

The tallest of the sailors sat with his shoulders against the rocks, his right arm looped into a sling made from his own neckerchief, while the other two lay, each with a pistol in his hand, peering at the hillside where our enemies were.

The boy turned to welcome us. 'We thank you for warning us,' he said, 'but you should not have joined us. They have us trapped here, I think.'

'That may be,' said Holmes, 'but we have four pistols between us. They have failed, so far, to inflict much damage from where they are. If they intend to finish us off, they will have to approach nearer, when we shall be able to cause them some little trouble. Is your aim as good now as it was on the jetty?'

The youth had the grace to blush. 'I am very sorry,' he said. 'We thought you were two of our enemies. Who are you, anyway?'

'Two gentlemen who are prepared to shoot in the same direction as you,' replied Holmes. 'Now, I suggest we watch the hillside very carefully.'

For nearly an hour we lay in the rocks, while our every move brought a fresh burst of firing from the slope across the stream. The sound of the guns and the whine of bullets put me in mind of my experiences of thirty years before, and I could not help wondering at the strange fate which had saved me from a Jezail bullet in the hills of Afghanistan only to leave me huddled on a Scottish moor dodging the bullets of the Kaiser's minions.

After a while the pattern of their firing seemed to change slightly. I peered cautiously at the trees, then grasped Holmes' arm.

'Holmes,' I said, 'I believe only three of them are still firing!'

Holmes listened for a while to the sound of the rifles, then scanned the slope with his glasses. 'You are quite right, Watson,' he said, and he tapped the young sailor on the shoulder.

'Do you see that clump of brush, some half-way from the stream to their position? Do you think you could put a shot into it?'

'Da – yes,' said the boy, and, levelling his pistol carefully, placed a single shot in the area Holmes had indicated. His accuracy was rewarded by a guttural cry and a figure lurched from the shade of the clump and staggered down towards the stream before falling and lying still.

Holmes smiled thinly. 'A first success to us, I think,' he said. 'Now let us see how they propose to winkle us out of here!'

The loss of one of their number seemed to dishearten the riflemen, for their firing grew more sporadic, but there was still no opportunity for us to escape from our position. Soon we became aware that the firing points had shifted, and that each of our enemies was separately working his way down the slope towards us. I drew Holmes' attention to the pattern.

'Yes,' he replied, 'But they will not be within the sensible range of our pistols until they reach the far side of the stream. Then, I fancy, things will become very interesting!'

Our occasional pistol shots did not stop their advance down the tree-covered slope, and soon we could tell that our enemies were right at the lower edge of the wood. We were reloading all of our weaponry, in readiness for their assault across the stream, when we heard the twin booms of a shotgun.

Our enemies spilled from the shade of the trees into the open, turning to fire wildly back at something in the wood behind them. Several shotguns blasted and one of them fell, while out of the shade of the wood erupted some six men, each armed with a double-barrelled piece.

We had scarcely grasped this new development when another of our enemies fell, and the lone survivor flung away his rifle and held up his hands. We got cautiously to our feet as he surrendered and observed the strange relief column that had rescued us. It seemed to consist of local men and youths, clad it tweed and tartan, with some in kilts. The stealthy skill with which they had crept down on the Kaiser's men suggested that they were ghillies or gamekeepers of the area, well used to silent stalking.

In our excitement we had forgotten to take account of our rear. Suddenly a harsh voice spoke behind us.

'Just put the wee pistols down quietly, gentlemen, and there'll be nae trouble!'

We whirled around, to find ourselves facing another party of armed ghillies, led by a stout, red-haired man with a broad beard. As we turned, he lifted the barrels of his shotgun threateningly.

'The pistols, gentlemen!' he repeated.

We placed our pistols on the ground as his men closed around us.

Holmes said, 'I am Sherlock Holmes and –'

'Aye! And I'm Rabbie Burns! Be so good as to stop your rattle, gents. You're a' oor prisoners!' growled the red-beared man. 'Alex, Ian, tie their hands so they'll gie us nae trouble. I'm thinking himself will want to weigh this catch in pairson!'

12

THE KING'S MESSENGER

All of us except the injured sailor had our hands bound behind us with stout cord by two of the ghillies, while the party from across the stream reported that three of the attackers were dead, two by shotgun and one by the young sailor's pistol shot. Their bodies were slung to poles without ceremony and, urged by the guns of our captors, we set out across the heather, six of us as captives and the dead riflemen carried behind like trophies of the hunt. Our guards looked so formidable and bore such a fearsome array of weaponry it would have been the veriest fool who tried to break away.

We tramped in silence up the northerly glen. From time to time, when I stole a glance at Holmes, I was surprised to see a slight smile playing around his mouth.

An hour's march brought us to the far end of the glen. It was now early evening and the sun was low between the hills to our left, reddening towards the day's end. As we came to the head of the valley Holmes, who was then slightly ahead of me, chuckled quietly. I looked ahead to see what had provoked his unlikely reaction and saw, its fairy-tale turrets lit by the westering sun, the Castle of Balmoral, the Scottish seat of our King.

Holmes has often, and sometimes fairly, accused me of not analysing the data in my possession, but now the explanation of our extraordinary adventures in Scotland began to dawn on me. Finding that a Russian vessel lay in a quiet Scottish harbour told him that the King's Russian contact had returned. He had guessed that Balmoral was their destination and accurately predicted the point where they were most at risk of an attack from the Kaiser's agents. I admit that the realisation that the guns around me were in the hands of Scotsmen loyal to King Edward comforted me considerably.

At the castle we were marched into a rear entrance and kept guarded in a stone-flagged room near the kitchens while lamps were lighted. Still at gunpoint we were taken down a flight of steps into a windowless underground area and ordered into a large, empty room, devoid of furniture but equipped with a stout door. Once inside we were ordered to lie on the floor, then our guards withdrew and we heard the sound of heavy bolts being secured on the other side of the door.

In the darkness that enveloped us I spoke Holmes' name, but he urged me to await events in silence. The Russians were whispering in their own tongue, and the surviving German was maintaining the silence he had kept since his capture.

How long we remained in darkness I do not know, for total obscurity has a tendency to distort the passage of time, but it seemed to be about half an hour before we heard the bolts being drawn outside. Four of our captors had returned and now ordered the German and the Russians to their feet, then marched them out of our prison.

'What is going to happen to us, Holmes?' I asked, when we were alone.

'Why, Watson,' he replied lightly, 'sooner or later His Majesty will realise the identity of his unexpected guests and we shall be released, I imagine.'

He had barely spoken the words when the door was opened again, to admit two servants with lamps, followed by a third person. I do not believe I have ever suffered such deep embarrassment as when a throaty chuckle issued from behind the lamps and there stepped into the lamplight the portly, bearded figure of our King.

His Majesty took the cigar from his mouth and stood for a moment, smiling at our predicament.

'Well, Mr Holmes,' he said at last, 'in the past when I have called upon you in connection with indiscretions of my own or my friends', it is I who have felt a little embarrassed. I trust that the balance is now restored.'

'Your Majesty has never had the least cause to feel embarrassed in my presence,' said my friend. 'It has always been an honour to be of service to any member of your family, and I trust that you will believe me when I say that the presence of myself and Dr Watson in your cellar arises only out of our desire to preserve the peace of your realm.'

'I do not doubt it, Mr Holmes, and I apologise for the scant respect with which my staff have handled you. I told my faithful ghillies to bring in any foreigners they found upon the castle lands. Unfortunately I failed to realise that, as Scotsmen, they might interpret that term as including Englishmen!'

He drew a watch from his pocket and turned it towards the lamp. 'My servants here will see you to rather more comfortable quarters, gentlemen, while I delay dinner a little. I will expect you in the drawing-room in one hour.'

The King withdrew and we were soon freed and established in two large, adjacent bedrooms in a distant part of the castle. Suitable clothing was made available to us and, within the hour, we were refreshed, if still tired from the day's exertions, when we made our way to the drawing-room.

The King soon joined us, in company with a tall, bearded man in the uniform of a Russian admiral carrying his right arm slung in a silk scarf. He was evidently one of the Russian sailors, but there walked at his side a tall and exceedingly graceful young woman. Her dark eyes glowed more brightly than the jewellery in her hair and her features were disturbingly familiar.

'Ah, gentlemen!' said His Majesty. 'Now that you have recovered from that somewhat discourteous reception, let me present to you His Imperial Excellency the Grand Duke Alexei and Miss Emily Norton, trickshot artiste and masculine impersonator of the American vaudeville circuits! Mr Sherlock Holmes and Dr Watson!'

Holmes had turned pale at the sight of the lady and now, as she smiled and reached out a hand, he stammered, 'Miss Norton? I don't understand . . . I –'

She interrupted him with a thrilling chuckle. 'Good evening, Mr Sherlock Holmes!' she said, her eyes sparkling with mischief.

My friend took her hand as though in a dream. 'That voice!' he said. 'You can only be –'

'Yes, indeed,' she interrupted him. 'The only daughter of the late Irene Norton, née Adler. I believe you were present at my parents' wedding, Mr Holmes, so I have more to thank you for

78

than saving my life this afternoon,' and she burst into outright laughter at my friend's bewilderment.

As the King joined in the laughter Holmes recovered his self-possession. 'Am I not also', he asked, 'in the presence of Miss Eileen Neagle, Mr Jonathan Y. Samuel and, indeed, the ship's boy of a certain Russian yacht?'

She bobbed him a curtsy. 'How very perceptive you really are, Mr Holmes! Yes, I was all of those, but how did you guess?'

'I realised very early on that Miss Neagle and Jonathan Samuel were most probably the same person. If the American emissary was female, a male disguise while on land was a greater protection, not to mention the fact that no female could have met my brother at the Diogenes Club. I confess that I was not certain of the identity of the youth on the yacht, other than the fact that he was not a sailor.'

'Really?' she said. 'I thought my performance was pretty convincing.'

'Very nearly, Miss Norton, but you drew attention to your hands by flourishing a pistol at us, and showed me that they were too fine and pale to be the hands of a working sailor-boy. Also, though your Russian accent was very convincing, you persistently called your vessel "it", rather than "she", a natural error in one of your sex, but definitely not the usage of sailors anywhere. However, your artistry with the pistol very nearly convinced me that I was wrong.'

'I have apologised for that,' she said, 'and I can only add that if I have some of my late mother's talents I have also some of her sense of humour and occasionally take a situation a little too far,' and she blushed very prettily.

King Edward placed his hand fondly on the American girl's arm. 'Young Emily here has all her mother's looks, wits and talent and she's going to need them all tonight. Emily, you're the only rose in this patch of thorns at dinner. Shall we go in?' and taking her arm in his, he led us into the dining-room.

I believe it was from his frequent visits to France that King Edward acquired the habit of ending his dinner with coffee rather than port, so that the ladies had no need to withdraw. Be that as it may, Emily was still with us when, with her permission, the cigars had been cut and lighted, and the King leaned forward across the table and addressed Holmes.

'Now then, Mr Holmes,' he said. 'My mother always set great store by you and I have to admit you've never let me down either. You see and understand what everyone else misses. So what brings you to Scotland on young Emily's heels?'

'The pursuit of a murderer, Your Majesty,' my friend replied. 'The arrest of a brutal maniac who has slain forty innocent people, endangered the life of Miss Norton, and come perilously close to removing you from your throne, sir.'

'So your brother hasn't seen fit to involve you in the politics of all this?' asked the King.

'On the contrary,' said Holmes, 'my brother drew me into the matter as an agent of the railway companies, merely to confirm his suspicion that both the Plymouth and Edinburgh trains had been deliberately derailed. Once I was able to do so, he positively discouraged Watson and me from taking any further steps in the matter.'

'Then he must be more of a fool than I took him for!' said the King. 'Look here, Mr Holmes, you're a deal smarter than the average and you must have more than an inkling of what this is all about, or you couldn't have made such a timely appearance on the moor this afternoon. Now, you tell us what you know and I'll see if there's anything I can add. We need the best brains there are in this thing.'

Holmes glanced round the table, and the King intercepted the look.

'It's quite safe, Mr Holmes. I started it off, Emily knows it all and the Grand Duke knows most of it. As to the doctor, he's kept your secrets long enough, eh, doctor? Tell us your story, Holmes!'

Holmes recited his tale succinctly, explaining each clue and inference that had drawn him to the moors above Balmoral that day, while all around the table kept silent. Emily's pearly shoulders gleamed in the candle-light and her wonderful dark eyes never left my friend's face as he told of our experiment on the South-Western Railway. As Holmes outlined the course of that afternoon's battle on the moor, the King rolled his cigar in his mouth and glanced admiringly at Emily.

When Holmes had done, it was the King's turn to explain his side of the story.

'There is very little more than you have deduced,' he told

Holmes. 'Your brother has told you the truth about my efforts to keep my idiotic nephew Willy in his place, but it becomes increasingly difficult and I shan't last for ever. Before I go I want a network of alliances that even Wilhelm will be forced to respect. Now, I made my own running with the French and it seems to have worked well enough, but the Americans don't go much on kings, so I needed an intermediary. By chance I came across Emily, performing in Paris, and saw at once whose daughter she was. In the course of making her acquaintance I let her know something of the problem.'

'So I volunteered!' interjected Miss Norton.

'That was extremely courageous of you,' I said.

'Nonsense, doctor!' she replied. 'I am English and American by birth and I was brought up partly in Europe. I know France, Germany and Russia well and speak their languages. Added to which, in this day and age, very few people suspect a stage girl of having the brains to be an international courier, and what acting talent I have is a great help.'

'So,' continued the King, 'I enlisted Emily's help in approaching the Americans first, for if they were to back us we would be unassailable. However, the news she brought back this summer was not good. It seems that there is no one in American politics who will risk his career by saying a good word for us. Not long after that setback, Emily contacted us from Russia with news of possibilities there, and it was that message that sent your brother and me on the Edinburgh Mail that night. Fortunately we survived the wreck and fortunately again we are making progress with our Russian negotiations, which is what brings the Grand Duke here. As to your own importance to my plans, Mr Holmes, you are too modest. If you had not intervened this afternoon they would have been in disarray, to say the least!'

'I must also offer you my thanks for your warning today,' said the Grand Duke, 'and for your brave assistance. You certainly saved us all.'

'Thank you, Your Excellency,' said Holmes. 'Yours too is a family I have been able to assist before.'

'Nevertheless, Mr Holmes,' said King Edward, 'your mission creates a problem. I am the last to wish that the scoundrel who brought about the train wrecks should go unpunished, but I see a serious embarrassment to my plans if

81

you were to arrest him. What is your next move in the matter?'

'With Your Majesty's permission I should like to interrogate the surviving German,' said Holmes.

'That is easily granted,' said the King, 'and as to the disposal of your murderer when you catch him – for I have no doubt you will – I think you must leave that with me for a while.'

His Majesty turned the conversation into more general paths, reminiscing about the occasion in Brussels in 1900 when an anarchist youth had fired a revolver at him through the window of a train.

'Were you hurt?' asked Emily Norton.

'No, m'dear,' said the King. 'He was a fifteen-year-old lunatic, and would you believe that their courts let him off? Said he was too young to form any criminal intent! I sometimes think that we spend our time trying to achieve some peaceful balance among the nations of the world and one day some little idiot like that will take a pot-shot at the wrong prince or politician at the wrong time and bring the whole house of cards down around us!'

Holmes and I slept deeply that night, wearied by our amazing day. In the morning we shared with His Majesty one of the gigantic breakfasts for which his household was famous. He told us that Mycroft would arrive during the morning and the afternoon would be taken up in discussion between himself, the Grand Duke, Emily Norton and Mycroft. He suggested that Holmes might like to pass the afternoon in questioning the German prisoner, who was still occupying one of the castle's cellars.

I did not join Holmes in that exercise, but passed the afternoon in strolling the grounds and gardens of the castle until a gong summoned us all to tea. Both Holmes and the diplomatic party looked well satisfied with their afternoon, though Mycroft was visibly put out at the presence of Holmes and myself.

'What brought you here, Sherlock?' he hissed, under cover of the teatime conversation.

'A logical process of deduction, as I imagined you would realise,' said Holmes. 'Tell me, dear brother, are you not doing rather a deal of travelling these days? I hope your office is suitably generous with your travelling allowance!'

The King interrupted the two brothers. 'Mr Holmes,' he

asked, 'how did your conversation with our friend down-stairs go?'

'I have learned a little more,' replied Holmes. 'The man you have in captivity is a minor functionary of your nephew's Intelligence Service, retained because of his skill with a rifle and explosives. After a little persuasion he managed to remember an Englishman who works with their spies. For what it is worth, his description matches our man, but he also has a knowledge of the stars. Your prisoner does not know a name, but says this Englishman trained him and others in the use of explosives to destroy railway installations and during that time he learned that the Englishman spoke more than a little Spanish. These are all useful indicators which will help to narrow the field of my search, sir.'

'Good!' said the King. 'Then you can leave me to arrange the disposal of our friend down below, and tomorrow, before you leave, I shall give you my answer as to the other matter.'

Mycroft left by night, hurrying away to London before his absence from his accustomed haunts became too obvious, but Holmes and I stayed till the following afternoon, taking our farewells of the Russian party when they set out once more across the hills in their sailor garb. This time, though, they were guarded all the way by a force of Balmoral's redoubtable ghillies.

The King himself honoured us by coming out to the great stone porch that fronts the castle as we were leaving. He was about to wave us away in our carriage when he stepped close to Holmes.

'You are quite right, Mr Holmes. Your assassin must not go unpunished. On the other hand there must be no trial. I understand from Dr Watson's accounts that you sometimes take a little liberty with my laws – if you lay this miscreant by the heels you may deal with him as you think fit. Do you understand me?'

'Entirely, Your Majesty!' replied Holmes.

As we bowled away from the front of the castle I could not forbear to question Holmes.

'Surely,' I said, 'the King has given you a licence to kill!'

'It seems so, Watson. It seems so!' said Holmes, and smiled grimly.

13

EMILY AND THE ASTRONOMER

Before parting from Holmes I urged him to keep me informed as to his attempts to track down the astronomer, but he was never a frequent correspondent.

The autumn of 1906 passed and Christmas too. Before the New Year there was news of another rail disaster, this time in Scotland, and inevitably I wondered if our insane astronomer had any connection with the matter. However, from an early stage it seemed likely that the weather was the greatest culprit. The incident stirred me to write to Holmes, asking whether he had made any progress in tracking the railway maniac.

If I had expected a letter I was disappointed. A few days later I received, with a Sussex postmark, three cuttings from scientific journals. No commentary accompanied them, but each was marked with a date in Holmes' hand. They were all identical in wording:

SPANISH-SPEAKING ASTRONOMER required by Gentleman to translate marginal notes in copy of *Dynamics of an Asteroid*. Reply to Box—.

With them was a copy of a letter cut from one of the same journals:

Sir,
May I make use of your correspondence column to ask if any of your readers are skilled, not only in astronomy, but also in modern Spanish?

I have recently inherited, from a relative who died abroad,

84

what seems to be a proof copy of the late Professor Moriarty's *Dynamics of an Asteroid*. My late cousin (who spoke and wrote Spanish with ease) had written copious marginal notes in that tongue which is, alas, unknown to me.

If these notes are of any scientific significance, it would be a pity for them to remain unknown through my own ignorance of Spanish. My late cousin was a distinguished amateur of astronomy and may have held views on Moriarty's work which might help in the understanding of it.

It would be a kindness if any reader who is familiar with both astronomy and the Spanish language, or who knows of any person who possesses both skills, would contact me through the office of your publication, with a view to translating this material.

There would, of course, be adequate recompense if required.
Yours etc., R. Wilson, Sussex.

These served only to show that my friend was at work on the problem and the method he was adopting, not whether he was obtaining any results, and whetted my curiosity still further. Nevertheless, I heard no more for a long time. The year passed from winter to spring and summer, the King embarked upon a series of visits in Europe, first to Paris, then to Spain and Italy. It was widely rumoured that he intended to persuade the Italians to withdraw from the Triple Alliance with Germany and Austria, and there was discussion of a treaty between Britain and Russia.

It was high summer once more when Emily Norton's efforts bore fruit and the Anglo-Russian agreement was signed. Many, of course, greeted it as an unworthy alliance with a tyrant, and there was talk of the knout and the salt-mines, but most people seemed to recognise that it was a necessary step in securing the peace of Europe.

It was a wet Sunday evening in August and I was contemplating an early bed when my housekeeper answered the front door bell and returned with Holmes at her heels.

'Watson!' he cried. 'I have a taxi-cab at the gate – we are summoned!'

'Summoned?' I stammered, and he thrust a letter into my hand. It bore the royal crest and a message from a secretary:

Dear Mr Holmes,

I am commanded by His Majesty to inform you that he will expect you and Dr Watson to await his pleasure at the Great Western Railway Station at Windsor at ten o'clock on Sunday evening.

Accommodation has been arranged for you and Dr Watson at the Castle.

I am, Sir, your obedient servant . . .

'What on earth is this all about?' I grumbled, as I tried to gather my wits.

'I apologise for taking you by surprise, Watson, but the Sunday post is not all that it might be in rural Sussex. As to what His Majesty requires . . . we shall see. In the mean time, our taxi awaits. If you will remove your slippers and smoking jacket and have a bag packed we can be in good time at Paddington.'

In minutes we were rattling away to the station. On the journey to Windsor Holmes spoke barely a word, merely gazing at the rain-sodden, twilit suburbs.

A porter tipped his cap to us as we alighted at our destination. 'Station master's compliments, gentlemen. Will you be so good as to follow me?'

He led us to an unmarked door and opened it, revealing a small, private waiting-room equipped with an ornate, mirrored sideboard. The scent of fresh tea cheered my nostrils and a musical voice with a pleasant American drawl met my ears. 'Why Mr Holmes and the doctor! Will you take tea?'

Emily Norton stood before us, looking radiant in a dress of striped silk.

'Miss Norton!' I said. 'What a very unexpected pleasure! Where on earth have you sprung from?'

She laughed attractively as she sat down. 'Oh we spies, doctor, we're almost as devious as consulting detectives. We have our methods, you know!'

'Wherever else you have been, Miss Norton, it is certain that you have recently been in Paris,' said Holmes.

'You even keep abreast of the fashion plates, Mr Holmes! My! But once again you hit the nail right on the head. The King sent for me from Paris and here I am.'

'I take it we are all here on the same business, but I thought your Russian adventures had been successfully concluded.'

'I told you before, Mr Holmes – I am half American and half English. I reckon that's a pretty good combination and I'm prepared to do anything I can to bring both my countries together.'

'So the negotiations in the United States are not over?' asked Holmes.

'With the politicians, yes. They're too scared of the voters to tell them anything but that any war is going to be a European war and their sons aren't going to Europe to bail out any King or Empire.'

'Then what other prospects are there, Miss Norton?' I asked.

'There are the money men, doctor. They know that a European war will be a long one and an expensive one and Britain will run out of money. Now, some of them think that's a good thing, that they can move in and take over all the overseas markets for British goods, but others have the sense to see that if Britain goes down and the Kaiser takes Europe, he'll want the world next.'

'Tell me,' I asked, 'Have these "money men", as you call them, sufficient influence on your politicians to force an alliance?'

'Not at present, doctor. There aren't enough of them and they aren't convinced it will go that far, yet. Still, there are one or two who see what's coming, and the next part of my job is to work on them to get an agreement that, if a war comes, they'll find money for Britain if she needs it.'

'With all possible respect,' said Holmes, and I knew that he meant it, 'that would seem a difficult task for you.'

'Oh, I don't know so much,' she said lightly. 'My Great-uncle Theobald is Chairman of the Evans Arizona Trust Bank. He's going to join us at Balmoral and my job on this trip is to see that he and the King get along.'

Holmes laughed delightedly. 'Miss Norton, with your mother's blood and that of one of America's greatest financiers in your veins, you are a formidable young lady indeed!'

A discreet knock heralded our porter, who showed us out of the station to a closed carriage waiting under the great glass canopy. It was now full dark and the rain had not slackened but, as we pulled away from the station I was aware that we had turned away from the castle.

I did not mention my misgivings, but as our route took us through meaner streets I began to wonder if we had not fallen into the hands of our adversaries. My unease mounted as we turned into the tall gates of a yard in a narrow back street.

Our driver took us inside a large and shabby carriage-house and pulled up. Holmes sprang out and helped Emily to the ground.

'Holmes,' I said, as I stepped down, 'are you sure we are not being decoyed?'

He laughed at my fears. 'Come, Watson,' he said, 'we are merely being required to use the spies' entrance to the castle,' and he led us through a door and into a gaslit passage.

A very few yards along the passage brought us to a wide and well-lit flight of steps, where four might go abreast. The stairs were cut from the very chalk and evidently of great age. As I gazed about me, Holmes laughed again.

'We are in the heart of the castle mound,' he said. 'King Edward is not the first of his line to need a discreet entry to his stronghold.'

Sure enough, we soon emerged into the private dwelling of one of the chaplains, within the walls of the castle, where a footman met us and escorted us to apartments in the royal living quarters.

We did not meet our host until breakfast the next morning, when he apologised for having had us smuggled into the castle.

'After our problems at Balmoral last year, it seemed to me that I should be very careful about any meetings connected with this affair,' he said. 'Now, gentlemen, I dare say you're wondering what this is all about?'

We confirmed that we were, and he continued.

'There's a number of reasons why you're here. Firstly because I want to know how far you've got with tracing this damned maniac who wrecks trains, and secondly because we may have some further information about your astronomer chap. Those good enough reasons, gentlemen?'

'I have not, as yet, been able to identify the man,' said Holmes and he drew from his inner pocket copies of the cuttings he had sent me. 'I posted this advertisement and letter in the scientific press after our return from Scotland last year.'

King Edward read the cuttings in silence, then returned them to Holmes. 'Had any results?' he asked directly.

'I believe that I have now assembled a list of every Spanish-speaking astronomer, whether professional or amateur, in the whole of your kingdom, sir. Over the past few months I have been making occasions to visit each, in a variety of different guises. By that means I have been able to eliminate those who are too young or too old, whose appearance is wrong or who were not able to be at Temple Combe or Peterborough on the relevant dates.'

'And do you believe that the murderer is among those who answered your advertisement, Mr Holmes?'

'Not necessarily, but my list also included those who were mentioned to me by others. I think he is more likely to be among those.'

'How many are left on your list?' asked the King.

'About a dozen who match what description we have and who had the opportunity, as far as I can ascertain. In addition there are some half a dozen who have been mentioned to me by others but did not themselves respond to my advertisements.'

'Then what's the next move?'

'To try to discover which of the men on my list have any knowledge of railways, explosives, or both, or any connection with Germany.'

'I don't envy you, Mr Holmes,' said the King, 'but I'm sure you will succeed in the end. Has Emily told you what she knows about your man?'

'No,' said Holmes, and we both turned to our fellow guest.

'Tell me again what you know about the astronomer,' she requested.

'We know only that he is of medium height, build and colouring. He is probably an educated Englishman. He speaks Spanish and may have been a railway or mining engineer. The colour of his eyes we do not know, nor whether his beard is false, but we reasonably suppose him to be an astronomer.'

'Well, I think I can assure you that the beard is real, Mr Holmes, and his eyes are brown.'

'Really?' ejaculated Holmes. 'May I ask how you know these things?'

'As you saw, I've been in Paris, performing there. Now an awful lot of gentlemen send their cards round to the dressing-room afterwards. I guess if I wanted I could dine out four or five times a night after the show. Well, one night in July I had a card from an English gentleman. Pierre, the doorman, said he was a decent sort of fellow, which I suppose means he tipped generously, and I let the Englishman take me out on the town.'

'What was he like?' asked Holmes.

'He was like your description, Mr Holmes. He was a man of middle height, about thirty-five years, medium colouring, brown eyes, with a beard much after the fashion of His Majesty's.'

'And what makes you believe he was our astronomer?' Holmes enquired.

She smiled. 'You must understand that these gentlemen who entertain lady artistes give us some really terrible lines of romance, Mr Holmes. At some point in the evening I asked him why he was taking me out. Well, he handed me a line about I was a star and stars were his special study. I thought he was just saying that, but he was right.'

'How do you know, Miss Norton?'

'We dined at a place with a terrace. It was a beautiful night and, while we were eating, he identified the stars to me. He knew all their proper names, and told me all sorts of things about them.'

'That does not make him our astronomer, Miss Norton,' said Holmes. 'Many people are familiar with the stars. What else was there?'

'Only that he spoke Spanish. The proprietor of the restaurant is Spanish, and this gentleman spoke to him in his own language.'

'Ah! That is better!' said Holmes. 'I think you do not speak Spanish yourself?'

'Only a few words from America, so I could not tell what was said, but the proprietor laughed with him about something. I asked him what it was and he said that the restaurant owner said his Spanish was good but he learned it in South America. Apparently they speak it differently there.'

'Of course!' cried Holmes. 'South America, the railway builders! Watson, remember how our engineers built railways all over South America a few years ago? That is where the ability with explosives comes from. He is an engineer or some such who has worked on the South American railways. Yes, Miss Norton, I begin to believe you are right, this is our man!'

'He said he was an engineer,' said Miss Norton, 'but I did not believe him.'

'Why not, pray?' said Holmes.

'His hands, Mr Holmes. Engineers work with them and it shows. This man had the hands of a gentleman who never used them for more than carrying a fancy cane.'

'You are an excellent observer, Miss Norton, and I am sure you are right, but he may have had some administrative connection with railways in South America. Tell me, do you still have his card?'

'Yes, surely. I brought it for you.' She searched in her handbag and produced it for my friend.

'Clifford Broughton, 14 Rue de Sainte Merise, Paris,' read Holmes. 'Probably as false as Mr Miller's address in London turned out to be, but I will have it checked. Why do you think he contacted you?'

'I really don't know. I suppose it may have been coincidence, but I asked Pierre if he had ever seen the gentleman before at the stage door and he said not. If it was your man, Mr Holmes, I think he was looking me over.'

'I have always found it difficult to believe in coincidence,' said Holmes. 'Where two elements of the same matter manifest at the same time there is almost always a connecting reason. I am very much afraid that the reason here may be that the Kaiser's agents have become aware of your involvement in His Majesty's negotiations. You must go carefully, Miss Norton, and we must see that you are not exposed to unnecessary danger.'

'Very true, Emily,' said the King. 'You will travel with my own party to Balmoral and I shall see you are protected there. Now, Holmes, doctor, I have one more guest arriving, who earnestly wishes to meet you, if you will stay for dinner tonight.'

'In the mean time,' suggested Emily, 'perhaps I may look at your list of astronomers and see if I can help in any way?'

14

KNAVE AND JOKERS

'Well, gentlemen,' said Emily, as we gathered around a table in the castle's library, 'we are all agreed on what the astronomer looks like. We believe his hobby is astronomy, he speaks English like a gentleman and Spanish like a South American, he has some practical knowledge of explosives and a possible connection with railways. He has claimed to be an engineer, but I beg leave to disbelieve him. Where do we go from here?'

'Admirably put,' said Holmes.

'But we still have not the slightest idea of where he is or who he really is!' I said.

'We have several possibilities,' said Holmes, and drew from his pocket some folded sheets of foolscap. 'Here are the names of those who answered my advertisements, some twelve of them, together with the names which I was given of persons who combine a knowledge of Spanish with an interest in astronomy.'

'Can we go through them?' asked Emily.

'Of course,' said my friend. 'There were others who contacted me, but my eliminations have left me with eighteen names and a few facts gleaned from various sources.'

'Who's first?' asked the young lady.

'They are in no particular order,' said Holmes, 'but the first is a Father James Gallagher of Saint Patrick's House, Wilversall in Staffordshire. I assumed from his title, patronymic and parish that he was of the Roman persuasion, in which I was right. The appropriate directory reveals that he is forty years old, educated in Ireland, entered the great Catholic seminary at Oscott near Birmingham and, apart from duties in Midland parishes, was some time with the Missionary Society of Saint

Joseph of Cupertino in South America. He is first on my list, but not first in my considerations.'

'Why not, Holmes?' I enquired.

'While he almost certainly speaks South American Spanish, he most probably speaks English like an Irish gentleman. Still, I shall find an occasion to visit him and clear up the point. The next name is another Celt, a Mr Gordon Macleod of Skye Cottage, Upavon in Wiltshire. My informant who recommended him tells me that Macleod is in his late thirties and a poet. He has published a number of works at his own expense, including *A Coronet of Stars* and *An Astronomer in Spain*. Him also I do not regard as a very likely suspect.'

'Is not Upavon only a short distance from Temple Combe?' I asked.

'So I believe, Watson, but it is a very great distance from Peterborough. I do not think his place of residence will help us very much. I have left him alone because of assumptions about speech. Even if he does not speak English with the lilt of his native island of Skye, he has travelled in Spain and his Spanish is likely to derive from this side of the Atlantic. The next may be more promising.'

'Who is that?' asked Emily.

'A secretive gentleman, whose first name has not been given me. I have him as Mr A. Alvarez. He lives at Manningham Towers, Hampstead – apparently in some style – but his country of origin, his occupation and the source of his wealth are unknown to those who know him in astronomical circles. His knowledge of the subject, revealed in correspondence, impresses them, but they know nothing more.'

'He might be Mexican with that name,' suggested Emily.

'A good thought,' said Holmes. 'His secretiveness, and his wealth, may have to do with the somewhat volatile politics of that country.'

'Do you think him significant?' I asked.

'Before answering that I shall have to look at the gentleman, Watson. If, as I suspect, he has the dark complexion and black hair of Spanish America, he cannot be our man. Of the next man on the list I know only that his name is Arthur Kelly, that he lives in Selwood Road, Willesden, and that he holds some office under the London County Council.'

'Not a great deal to go on,' commented Emily.

'No,' said Holmes. 'Another occasion, I suppose, for my pose as an itinerant preacher or a door-to-door pedlar of trifles. Next I have Dr George Scorfeld, who teaches science and languages at an academy for young men in Pawsley, Hampshire. At present that is all I know of him.'

'A German name, perhaps?' queried Miss Norton.

'Perhaps,' agreed Holmes, 'but an English Christian name – still, maybe he is of mixed parentage. On the other hand, I discount him because he teaches languages and most probably speaks Spanish correctly. I know nothing of the next man, save that his name is Alan Lennox and he lives at Staddeley Manor Farm in the West Riding of Yorkshire and is a member of a number of astronomical societies. Next is a candidate I have not seriously considered, Miss Priscilla Debenhoe, whose address was given to me as in care of the Working Ladies' Settlement in Whitechapel. I think we may leave the lady to her work, on the assumption that she almost certainly lacks Miss Norton's skills,' and he smiled at Emily.

'If I really met the astronomer in Paris,' said Emily, 'I can assure you that he was not Miss Debenhoe in disguise. You can leave out the ladies, if there are any more.'

'Then we come to a Mr Manuel Pereira, an importer of indiarubber. He has a gutta-percha manufactory, the Eagle Works, in Deptford. He, presumably, speaks Spanish in the South American fashion, but I imagine, as in the case of Mr Alvarez, that however perfect his English, his appearance will exclude him. There is Nathaniel Bramwell, a gentleman who keeps stud horses at The Birches, Wokingham and who has published *The Architecture of the Universe*, and at Stoke Mohun in Dorset the vicar is the Reverend Oliver Corlett, author of *Stars of Catalonia* and *The Candles of Montserrat*.'

'Is Montserrat not a West Indian island?' I asked.

'Indubitably, but I believe the reverend gentleman's work to refer to the ancient monastery of Montserrat in Catalonia. Again, I doubt that he is our man, as he will speak either pure Castilian Spanish or the Catalan variant.'

'Do you really believe he is somewhere in your list?' said Emily.

'If he is, indeed, an astronomer who speaks Spanish, then he should be,' replied Holmes. 'Perhaps he is Mr Percival Sheldon, who lives in Sydenham and is a clerk to a firm of import and export agents in Deptford.'

'Foreign contacts,' said Miss Norton. 'What do they import and export?'

'Almost anything on which there is a profit to be made, I imagine,' said Holmes, 'and they may well have connections with Germany, not to say Aberdeen and Plymouth. I shall, I think, look into Mr Sheldon's affairs. Now we have a barrister-at-law, Mr Edmund Sinclaire of the Temple and Siddenton Manor in Hampshire.'

'Isn't Siddenton one of those little hamlets in northern Hampshire?' I asked.

'Your schoolday memories serve you well, Watson. I looked it up in the Railway Guide to Hampshire. It is on the Didcot and Southampton line. The guide says that the house lies at the foot of the downs and was formerly the home of Vernon Coxe, the Hampshire poet. There are chalk-pits in the vicinity from which many interesting fossils have emerged. The next suspect is, I think, more interesting. He is of your profession, Watson.'

'Really? Who is he?'

'He is Dr Henry Barton of Lawes Road, Doncaster. He specialises in tropical diseases and ophthalmic surgery and has published papers on "Diseases of the Amazon Basin" and "Hazards of the Iron-Welding Trade", as well as one book – *A Doctor on the Amazon River.*'

'The engine-men of the Edinburgh express came from Doncaster,' I observed.

'So they did, but that is not why he interests me. I am intrigued by the fact that he spent six years in South America with the Anglo-German Medical Mission.'

'A German connection and a South American connection!' said Miss Norton.

'Exactly!' said Holmes. 'I think I must call on Dr Barton in the very near future. There is also Captain Lymington-Keith, who lives at Braemar in Scotland. He is unmarried and, according to the Army List, served with distinction with the Engineers in South Africa and withdrew from the Army upon inheriting his estate. I find him interesting.'

'Apart from the location of his estate, I don't see why he is more interesting than some of the others,' I remarked.

'Really, Watson – and you an ex-soldier! Have you forgotten that both railways and explosives lie within the field of military engineers?'

'What's the significance of his estate?' asked Emily.

'Only that it lies close to the King's lands at Balmoral,' replied Holmes.

'Explosives, railways, the Balmoral connection.' Emily counted them off on her elegant fingers. 'Yes, Mr Holmes, I think he should go to the top of your list!'

'Not to mention a possible German connection,' said Holmes.

'I don't see it,' I said.

'It is only a possibility,' said Holmes, 'but the South African war was encouraged by Germany. She supplied "advisers" to the Boers in the field and her spies were everywhere. If the Captain has betrayed his commission, South Africa may well have been where he was recruited.'

'I cannot', I said, 'believe such behaviour possible in a man who has held the Royal Commission!'

'It is a cardinal error, Watson,' said Holmes, 'to project your own virtues, or indeed your own vices, on to another. It cannot be said that every man who has held a commission has had your own sturdy patriotism. However, we have not done. There is Mr Anthony Edwardes of Windraw House, Grindling, Suffolk. He owns a fleet of barges working the east coast and the North Sea, and is himself a distinguished amateur yachtsman – author of *A Seaman's Manual of the Heavens*.

'A European connection again,' said Emily.

'Yes,' said Holmes, 'but if he is a regular yachtsman he would hardly have the unmarked hands of your Parisian admirer. Still, I shall look at the gentleman. I think I should also pay attention to James Fuller of Fuller's Wharf at Harwich. He is a timber trader to the Baltic, and also in the wine-shipping trade from Spain and Portugal. His Spanish may be pure or not, but he also has European connections.'

He scanned his notes again. 'Finally there are two whom I regard as of very little interest – Miss Myfanwy Morgan, an erstwhile teacher of languages and handicrafts to young ladies, who now operates the Practical Handicrafts Shop in

Aldgate, and an Arthur Brown of Stanton's Hotel, Charing Cross.'

'What does Mr Brown do?' I asked.

'He composes music-hall songs, of which he was kind enough to forward me some copies. I have not brought them with me, but their titles I note as "A Lady from Spain on a Train", "In Old Barcelona" and "My Rose of the Ramblas", from which I infer that Mr Brown's Spanish will be Castilian or Catalan.'

'With the exception of the Doncaster doctor and the Scottish captain, there does not seem much indication against any of them,' said Emily. 'How will you proceed now, Mr Holmes?'

'I shall carry on finding occasions to visit each of these persons, in one guise or another. You must realise, Miss Norton, that there will be a great deal more to each of them than my notes reveal, and I have little doubt but that eventually I shall knock at the door of our murderous astronomer.'

'Surely that will take some time, Holmes?' I commented.

'It must, Watson, it must. I assembled these lists from the relatively small and enclosed world of astronomy enthusiasts in Britain. Like all small groups, they gossip. Our maniac knows someone is on his trail. I cannot afford to start a train of speculation in his narrow community by being precipitate. I must move slowly.'

'Is there no quicker way?' asked Emily.

'I will, of course, take such assistance as Mycroft's department can offer, but at present that seems little. Had my bureaucratic brother not allowed the traditions of the Civil Service to overrule his native intelligence this man would never have struck twice. Had he communicated his suspicions to me after the Salisbury catastrophe we would have been ready for him at Peterborough, but now I must do it the long, hard way.'

We closed our conference and changed for dinner. When we met later in the drawing-room His Majesty introduced us to Theobald G. Evans, Emily's financier uncle. I had come to expect Americans, especially Westerners, to be large men, often with an unusual taste in dress, but the great banker was a short, stocky man. He carried a thick mane of silver hair and heavy side-whiskers, between which two shrewd blue eyes looked out of a weather-beaten countenance. He was dressed in sober black.

'I must thank you both', he said, once the introductions had been effected, 'for looking out for Emily. His Majesty tells me that you got her out of a nasty scrape in Scotland last summer. I've followed your doings in Lippincott's for a good many years now, but I never thought my great-niece would be rescued by the world's greatest detective.'

'Miss Norton is a plucky and resourceful lady in her own right,' said Holmes.

'It was an honour, Mr Evans,' I said.

He laughed again. 'You British amaze me,' he said. 'You get into someone else's gunfight and you call it an honour! All I can say is that you both have my marker and if you ever call upon it I'll be happy to help you in any way that I can.'

'You are very kind,' said Holmes. 'May I ask if Miss Norton returns to the States with you?'

'We have not seen that far ahead. Why do you ask?'

'If she does not travel with your party, she should take especial care. She should not, for example, travel from Glasgow or Liverpool.'

'Why not, Mr Holmes?' asked the banker.

'The Kaiser's agents discovered her presence in Britain twice last year. The same may occur again. I merely suggest she avoids the obvious ports for the States to elude danger. She should probably steer clear of Plymouth too, since we believe the All Highest has an agent in that city.'

Holmes and I left Windsor after dinner, by the same subterranean route that had brought us. As we made our way through the ancient tunnel I asked Holmes, 'Do you really believe that Emily is in danger?'

'She may be in very great danger indeed,' he replied, and I shuddered at the thought of that brave and bright young lady in the clutches of a monstrous killer.

THE SHREWSBURY HORROR

It was not so long before Holmes contacted me again. One morning in mid-October my housekeeper brought to my breakfast table a telegram from him. As usual, it explained nothing. It said:

> JOIN ME EUSTON STATION THREE TOMORROW FOR SHORT TRIP TO SHROPSHIRE STOP HOLMES

I was, of course, at Euston on the next day, filled with anticipation and curiosity. I could not know that our journey to Shropshire would thrust us into the heart of the horrors created by the railway maniac.

Once our train was well on its way north I questioned Holmes as to the purpose of our journey.

'I have had this from Mycroft,' he said, and passed me a telegram.

It had been handed in at the village post office at Ballater, by Balmoral, and read:

> JONATHAN Y SAMUEL SAILS FROM BRISTOL DAY AFTER TOMORROW STOP FIRST STAGE OF AMERICAN DEALINGS PROMISING STOP PRISONER FRANCIS MILLER HELD AT SHROPSHIRE COUNTY GAOL MAY BE YOUR STARGAZER STOP GOVERNOR EXPECTS YOU 10 PM TOMORROW STOP M

'What do you make of it, Holmes?' I asked.
'Very little, at present. I know that Theobald Evans left

Balmoral last week, because the newspapers reported his arrival in Zurich some days ago, which explains why Miss Norton is travelling alone. I am pleased to note that the King's negotiations are proceeding well, and just as pleased that my advice as to Miss Norton's travelling arrangements has been heeded.'

'But the prisoner Miller, Holmes – can he be our man?'

'The cleverest of villains makes silly mistakes, Watson,' he replied. 'Our railway murderer has twice used the same alias, to our knowledge. He may have used it again, or it may even be his real name.'

'Then you think we may come face to face with him at last?'

'I think nothing, Watson! You are theorising in advance of the data once again. Francis Miller of Shrewsbury Gaol may be our man, or he may be a Shropshire poacher. We shall see.'

As the afternoon wore on we rattled north-west into the Midlands, coming eventually to that blighted and scarred landscape which the iron manufacturers and their associated trades have created around Birmingham and Wolverhampton. I have heard it said that Queen Victoria, when she passed through this area by rail, would have the carriage blinds drawn as the train approached Birmingham and not permit them to be opened until Wolverhampton was passed.

The region produced a most depressing effect, but this lightened as we travelled west, towards the Welsh border and our destination. Soon we could see the hills of the border on the horizon and knew that Shrewsbury was not far.

An enquiry at the railway station revealed that the prison lay close by, on the hill above the station. We climbed a stepped footpath beside the remains of the town's ancient castle, where a footbridge crossed the railway lines and carried us directly to the prison itself. If any of my readers are familiar with the great prisons of London, Birmingham or Manchester, they must not imagine anything so grimly impressive. Shrewsbury is not one of the huge city fortresses, but a small county gaol, built to serve the moderate needs of a rural area, and its small gateway and gatehouse are almost homely by comparison.

A ring at the bell quickly produced a warder at the wicket door, to whom Holmes explained our business. He let us in and

101

invited us to wait in the little gatehouse while he investigated our appointment with the Governor.

He was gone for no little time, eventually returning with a perplexed expression. 'Are you sure your appointment was for tonight, Mr Holmes? The Governor don't seem to know anything about it.'

Holmes confirmed that we had expected to see the Governor that evening, but the warder shook his head.

'Well, sir, the Governor hasn't been told about it. Still, if you dunna mind waiting a few minutes, the Major'll come and see about it hisself.'

The Governor joined us within a short time, full of apologies but nonplussed as to the reasons for our visit. Holmes' explanation left him none the wiser.

'We have no Francis Miller here at present. Miller is a common enough surname, and we have three of them, but none of them is a Francis. Is there a mistake in the name, do you think? What is your Francis Miller likely to have done?'

'Perhaps it would help', said Holmes, 'if you were kind enough to allow us to see all of your Millers?'

The Governor consented at once. Another warder was called to attend us and we were taken to the cells of each of the Millers in turn. A glance through the spy-hole of each cell was sufficient. The first was a youth of about seventeen, whose appearance suggested he was dimwitted, the second was a tall, thin, man with hair of jet black and the third was plump, balding and far too old to be our quarry.

On the way back from the third cell Holmes apologised to the Governor. 'I can only imagine', he said, 'that some clerk in my brother's office has blundered. Very likely the man we want is at Exeter or at Lincoln!'

The Governor was exceedingly polite about our unheralded arrival and our fruitless quest, and was concerned at our travelling arrangements. Holmes was anxious to travel back to London as soon as possible and the Governor suggested that we wait for the late Bristol train and catch a London express at Bristol. It would, he assured us, be more reliable than trying to travel back through the Midlands at a late hour. In the mean time, nothing would give him greater pleasure than to have us join him for supper in his quarters.

We accepted his advice and his invitation and supped agreeably in the Governor's comfortable suite in the gaol, where he and Holmes discussed the many theories as to whether criminals are born or made. When supper was over he walked us down to the gate, reminding us, as we left, of the route across the footbridge to the railway station.

We were crossing the bridge when I asked Holmes, 'Do you really believe that some assistant of Mycroft's has sent us on this fool's errand by a mistake?'

'No, Watson,' he replied. 'We have been decoyed, but I confess I cannot divine the purpose. Still, the journey through Bristol will give us more than enough time to ponder on the matter.'

He had scarcely spoken the words when he stopped dead. He turned to me, his eyes widening.

'The journey through Bristol!' he repeated. 'What fools we have been! Quickly, Watson! There is not a second to lose!'

He broke into a run and I, though not comprehending, ran after. Helter-skelter we tumbled down the steps beside the ruined castle and raced across the forecourt of the railway station. Holmes pounded into the the castellated entrance of the station, flashing our *laissez-passers* at an astonished ticket collector and, in a moment, we were on the main platform.

It was empty of people, apart from a group of postmen with a cart loaded with mailbags.

'The Bristol train!' Holmes shouted to them. 'Where is it?'

'Why, sir, she's just about due. You're all right, we're waiting for her!'

He had hardly spoken the words when a telegraph clerk ran out from the telegraph office, his face a white mask under the gas lamps. 'The Bristol's runnin' away!' he shouted. 'The box 'as signalled, she's runnin' away into the junction curve!'

As we stood frozen with horror, we heard the sound of the train beyond the station, heard its steady rhythm break, to be followed by a hideous, juddering, splintering sound that seemed to go on for ever.

Before the echoes of that dreadful sound had died away Holmes cried, 'Come Watson!' and set off at a run. I panted after him, wretched in the knowledge that we had heard the

103

Bristol Express derail itself and that a passenger on that train had been Miss Emily Norton.

It is ten years since Holmes and I ran along the platform at Shrewsbury to reach the wrecked express, and in recent times I have seen more than my fill of the human debris of modern warfare, the victims of high-explosive shells and of poison gas. I have dealt with survivors of the troop-train crash at Quintinshill, where more than two hundred soldiers died and where weeping officers drew their guns and shot men trapped in the blazing wreckage, but nothing will erase from my mind the impressions left on that October night in 1907.

The junction curve where the disaster had occurred is a bend in the main railway line from the north of only some six hundred feet in radius. To prevent derailments, no train was supposed to enter the curve at more than ten miles an hour, but, as we subsequently learned, the Bristol train had failed to stop at the first signal box for Shrewsbury and had run past and on to that deadly curve at sixty miles an hour or more.

The consequences had been inevitable. The express engine had failed to negotiate the bend, leapt from the rails and ploughed across the ground until it rolled on to its side, killing its hapless engine-men. As it came to rest, the fifteen carriages and wagons behind it, still travelling at awesome speed, slammed into it and into each other, mounding together in a hideous heap of splintered wood, broken glass and twisted metal – making that terrible shuddering, smashing sound we had heard from the station platform.

Holmes and I were among the first to arrive at the scene. Already people were clambering from the wreck, but the cries that echoed in the night showed that many others were trapped in the broken mass. While Holmes leapt to the rescue of those still trapped I applied my medical skills to helping those who had emerged. There was no time to consider Miss Norton's fate, only to do whatever could be done for those who had been injured.

Other medical men soon arrived and we toiled together at the trackside, staunching wounds, bandaging and splinting, all too often finding that there was nothing our skill could do. By the flare of the lamps we mended broken limbs as best we could, against a background of cries and groans from the trapped and the sobbing of the injured. I learned later that, throughout the night, Holmes performed prodigies of strength and ingenuity in rescuing people from the wreckage.

With daylight a thin autumn mist seeped up from the Severn, mingling with the smoke from the wreck as though to blur the outlines of that nightmare scene. By then the living had all been removed, together with many of the dead. As I squatted wearily at the trackside, Holmes approached me and put into my hands an enamel mug of strong tea, laced with rum.

The hot tea and spirits reawakened my tired, horrified brain. 'Is there any news of her?' I asked my friend.

His face was as pale and as hard as a carving in alabaster. 'No, Watson,' he said. 'They say that there are a dozen passengers dead, but Miss Norton is not among them. Nor, as far as I can tell, is she among the survivors.'

'Then she may be safe?' I cried hopefully.

'She may be, old friend, but there may still be bodies to be freed from the wreck.' He laid a hand on my shoulder. 'Come,' he said. 'You have done all you can here. We must go to London and seek my brother.'

Of all the journeys we made in our pursuit of the railway maniac, none was more painful than our return to London. Exhausted by the night, I dozed fitfully, but each time I awoke I saw Holmes wide awake, his face a pale, stern mask, staring sightlessly out of the window. I knew that he was blaming himself for his failure to locate the Kaiser's madman and for his advice to Emily's great-uncle that she should not travel from Plymouth or a northern port. I, too, was numb with horror at the thought that such a gallant and charming girl might yet be lying in the smoking wreckage we had left behind.

We reached Euston far too early for Mycroft to be at his club, and made straight for his office. In the palatial lobby of the great Italianate building that houses the department a uniformed attendant took Holmes' card. What he can have made of our red-eyed faces and battered appearance I cannot imagine. He disappeared up a wide staircase and very shortly returned, requesting us to follow him. He led us through broad corridors to a double door, where he knocked and stood aside as we entered.

At the far end of a large room sat Mycroft at an imposing desk, silhouetted against a wide window. Behind him a second figure stood, looking out at the autumn sunshine on the yellowing treetops of St James's. At the sound of our entrance she turned and I felt my heart miss a beat.

'Miss Norton!' exclaimed Holmes and I as one.

'Why, gentlemen!' she said. 'How very nice to see you again so soon! Your brother never told me you were expected, Mr Holmes.'

'Only because he was not,' said Mycroft. 'Do have a seat, dear brother, and you too, doctor, and tell us what brings you into the corridors of state. Both of you look absolutely dreadful.'

'Have you not heard what has happened at Shrewsbury last night?' asked Holmes.

'I am afraid not,' said Mycroft. 'I usually leave the newspapers until I arrive at my club, they are so much better digested in silence. What has occurred at Shrewsbury?'

'The night mail from Scotland to Bristol and the West was destroyed by derailment on a curve outside Shrewsbury!' said Holmes bleakly.

Mycroft's pale grey eyes started and Miss Norton's hand flew to her mouth. She uttered a groan.

'Oh no!' she cried. 'They thought that I was on it!'

'I am afraid that is true,' said Holmes.

'How many died, Mr Holmes?' she asked, close to tears.

'Eleven passengers, the engine crew, two other railwaymen and three Post Office men – eighteen all told, bringing our assassin's total to fifty-eight. Do not blame yourself, Miss Norton. The fault is mine,' said Holmes. 'For more than a year I have known of this man and failed to stop him. Now he taunts me with my failure!'

'In what way?' asked Mycroft.

'By this,' said Holmes, taking out the telegram. 'By sending this so that he could guarantee I would be at the scene of his hideous handiwork!'

Mycroft took the telegram and examined it. 'This was not sent by me, nor by anyone with my authority,' he said.

'I do not doubt it,' replied Holmes, 'and thereby hangs another tale.'

We all looked at him questioningly.

'Do you not see?' he said. 'The Paris incident raised a strong

106

suspicion that the Kaiser's men were aware of Miss Norton's identity. Where did they obtain that knowledge? This telegram was sent by someone who knew of a plan to send Miss Norton by train to Bristol. Was there such a plan?'

'Yes,' said Mycroft. 'That was the way she would have travelled last night if she had been returning to the United States, but those arrangements were cancelled when she accepted an engagement to remain and perform in London.'

'Then you have one of the spies of the All Highest somewhere in your office!' said Holmes.

16

KING AND KNAVE

'You make a very grave imputation against the probity of my office!' said Mycroft.

'Not without warrant!' replied Holmes. 'The evidence is there, and was there before. I have been behind-hand in this. I should have seen much earlier the real significance of the Grantham disaster, but I was so concerned in establishing the identities of the two gentlemen at Peterborough that, when I succeeded, I failed to ask myself how our destroyer of trains knew that you were on that train, Mycroft.'

'Are you saying that the Grantham episode was aimed solely at me?' said Mycroft.

'Of course it was,' said Holmes. 'I'll wager that no one but you knew that His Majesty was to join you at Peterborough. Is that not so?'

'True.'

'Then the arrangements to halt the Edinburgh Mail were made by someone who knew you were leaving London, an event so extraordinary they linked it to the negotiations and moved to prevent your journey.'

'You make a good case,' said Mycroft thoughtfully, 'but if you are right, how will we trace our traitor?'

'You must take every precaution to ensure that information is reserved to the smallest number of persons possible. If there is any further misuse of information, the fewer who knew it the greater our chance of unmasking the traitor. In the mean time you must consider carefully what you know about all those who knew you were travelling to Scotland and all those who knew that Miss Norton was to travel to Bristol last night. There is, fortunately, a way of narrowing your search.'

'What is that?'

'By considering those who did not know that Miss Norton's arrangements had been cancelled. Only one of those can have passed the information.'

'These things will be done,' said Mycroft, 'but there is also the question of Miss Norton. If our madman has linked her to me and knows her movements, then she is in peril every moment she remains in England. Indeed, I cannot say that she will be safer in the United States. The Kaiser's Intelligence Service has been well organised there for a good many years.'

He drummed his fingers on the desk for a moment. 'There may be a way of protecting Miss Norton – if His Majesty will do it.'

He pressed a button on his desk and, pulling a sheet of paper towards him, began to scribble rapidly. It was only a few moments before a clerk knocked at the door and entered, but Mycroft's note was already finished and sealed.

'See that this goes to the Palace at once,' he told the clerk. 'It is not to go through the Registry, but directly to the Palace.'

Some three-quarters of an hour later we were at Buckingham Palace, where a liveried footman showed us into a large and handsome room set around with marble pillars, and assured us that His Majesty would join us shortly.

We had not waited long when a door opened and the King came in, clad informally in a smoking jacket. He waved us peremptorily back to our seats as we rose, and took an armchair opposite us.

'Well, Mycroft,' he said, 'your note spoke of the utmost urgency. What the devil's going on?'

'Your Majesty, my brother and Dr Watson have news of the railway catastrophe at Shrewsbury last night – news which threatens the safety of Miss Norton,' replied Mycroft.

'Then you'd better tell us about it, Mr Holmes,' said the King.

Briefly and starkly Holmes described the events of the previous night and the inferences he had drawn from them. The King listened in silence until he had finished.

'It sounds as if you're right, Mr Holmes,' he said, when my friend's narrative ended. 'Mycroft had better look to the people in his office and we had better take steps to safeguard Emily,' and he smiled at her.

'Sir,' said Mycroft, with more diffidence than I was used to from him, 'it seems to me that things have come to such a pass that the most stringent measures must be taken to stop this lunatic.'

'Easier said than done!' said the King. 'What are we to do – set the police looking for him all over the country? Pretty kettle of fish that would be! In no time at all we'd have let the cat right out of the bag, and what would the people think if they knew that some murderous imbecile in the Kaiser's pay had been going about the country wrecking trains and killing dozens of innocent people? There'd be no stopping them – they'd want a war, that's what they'd want, and I can't say I'd blame 'em!'

'With respect, sir, that is precisely my point,' said Mycroft. 'If Your Majesty was willing to present the facts we now have to the German Ambassador – not, of course, mentioning Miss Norton's part in all this – and point out to him that the operations of German Intelligence have given us an excuse for war at any time, might not that put a stop to this fiend's excesses?'

'You may be right,' said the King.

'Would your nephew believe that you were serious in your threat to use this excuse to make war upon Germany?' asked Holmes.

King Edward laughed heartily. 'Forgive me, Mr Holmes,' he said, 'but my nephew Willy would believe almost anything of me except the truth! He calls me the Encircler, in fact he held a public dinner in Berlin and told all his high-born guests that I was the Great Satan! No, Mr Holmes, there will be no difficulty in convincing Willy that I might seize any excuse to make war on him. I shall tell the German Ambassador that I am personally aware of the depredations of a criminal lunatic employed by Carlton House Terrace and that any further efforts in the same direction will lead to undeclared war. His master will believe every word of it!'

'Does not that place you at risk, sir?' I asked.

'No, doctor. There is a kind of gentlemen's agreement among kings and emperors, that we don't go around having each other assassinated. Puts us all at risk if any one of us started that, you see, and anyway, Wilhelm is still my nephew – he might not care for my politicking very much, but he won't see his old uncle off!'

'So we can stop the train-wrecker,' said Holmes, 'but Miss Norton will still be at risk. Unless . . .' and he paused.

'Unless I use the traitor in my office to protect her,' said Mycroft.

'How do you mean?' asked the King.

'If I ensure that my entire department knows that Miss Emily Norton was merely a blind, a misdirection, while others made the contacts, Your Majesty, then my traitor is bound to carry that information to his German masters and they will leave Miss Norton alone.'

'My thoughts exactly!' said Holmes.

'Good!' said the King. 'Emily, I'm sure Mycroft's plan will work and you may carry on as usual.'

We rose to leave, but the King halted us. 'One moment, gentlemen. We may have solved Emily's problems, but what of yourself, Mr Holmes? What will you do?'

'I, sir?' said Holmes. 'Why, I shall continue my enquiries, of course.'

'Do you not think that unwise?' asked His Majesty.

'Unwise, sir? I cannot believe it to be so.'

'Mr Holmes,' said the King, 'no one appreciates more than I the efforts you have made in this matter, and I share your belief that this lunatic must be dealt with, but I begin to fear that now is not the right time. My negotiations have no further need of Emily's courageous services, and I shall take the steps we have discussed to ensure her protection, but what can I do to protect you?'

'I do not believe that I entirely understand you, sir,' said Holmes.

'Mr Holmes, we can bring the astronomer's operations to a stop, but we cannot identify him. You do not know him, but he already knows that you are seeking him. That puts you at a disadvantage if you come upon him. He will expect you. Further, if his masters at Carlton House Terrace frustrate his other activities, might he not seek vengeance on you?'

'These are risks which I am prepared to take, sir,' said Holmes.

'I am sure that you are,' said the King, 'but I am not prepared to let you take them. You have been too valuable to my family personally, to my Throne as an institution, and to numbers of my subjects, for me to allow it. Rest assured that so long as I live I shall not forget the crimes this man has committed, and the time will come when I shall ask you to pursue him again, but that will be when he least expects it. For the present I rely on your loyalty when I ask you to suspend your enquiries.'

Holmes' face was a mask. 'Very well, sir. If that is what Your Majesty wishes, then that is what I shall do.'

'I do wish it, Mr Holmes, and I am grateful for your loyalty to my wishes.'

When we were alone in a cab, I asked my friend what he would now do.

'You heard the King, Watson. It is fruitless to spend time in thinking about what cannot be achieved. I shall return to my bees until I receive His Majesty's command.'

He said nothing more till we arrived at Victoria, where he took a curt farewell of me. I knew, of old, his frustration at incomplete cases, and as I watched him stride away I felt deeply sorry for my old friend. Even so, I do not suppose that either of us believed that the King's command would never come.

17

SPADE AND JOKER

'As long as I live . . .' King Edward's words echoed in my head as I stood with the two Holmes brothers on a balcony of Mycroft's department, nearly three years later. It was a hot, bright morning with a cloudless summer sky, but the face of the capital was shadowed by the dark-clad crowds that had gathered to see their King go to his last rest. The muffled drums and the slow tread of marching feet could still be heard as we turned back into the stately room behind the windows.

'Who knows', I murmured to Holmes, 'what thoughts are running in the Kaiser's head this morning, as he sees the man who outwitted him for ten years carried to his grave!'

'That is easy,' said Mycroft. 'The madman even took the opportunity of the Funeral Banquet last night to tell the French Ambassador that France should side with Germany if there is war with Britain!'

'Then there does not seem to be any "if" about it,' said Holmes. 'The only question left is "when?".'

We were interrupted by a black-garbed footman, who showed Miss Norton into the room. She was in deep mourning and beneath her veil her eyes were reddened.

'Oh, gentlemen,' she said, and there were tears still in her voice. 'How beautiful, but how sad!'

'He was not young,' ventured Mycroft, ushering us to where his staff had laid a small buffet.

'Oh, I know,' she said, 'but he was so full of life and ideas! And how the people loved him – they wept out there as if they knew him personally. They called him Teddy, like a favourite uncle.'

'The newspapers called him "The Uncle of Europe",' said

Mycroft, 'and it was near enough true. Apart from his nephew Willy, the Czar was his nephew and the Czarina his niece. The Queen of Norway was his daughter and the Queen of Spain another niece, and where he wasn't related to a Royal Family himself they were related to his wife.'

The attendants had poured wine for us. Mycroft lifted a glass.

'Ah well,' he said, 'King Edward is on his way to Paddington and into the history books. Long live King George!'

We raised our glasses and drank in silence.

'I take it you believe war is now inevitable?' asked Holmes.

'It is, as you say, only a question of when. The Kaiser both feared and respected his Uncle Edward – cousin George he calls "a nice young man". When he is ready he will drag all Europe into war.'

'But there is a growing opinion that war between the civilised nations is impossible,' I said.

'Idealistic nonsense!' snapped Mycroft. 'It has no more reality than the belief that yesterday's comet foretold a war. Oh, we have had sixty years of peace in Europe, but when war comes it will be appalling. Look at America – at their Civil War. That ingenious nation showed us the outline of modern war, with balloons and undersea boats, ironclads and starvation sieges. If the European nations turn their factories to war production the result will be dreadnoughts and flying machines by the hundred, zeppelins and long-range cannon, submersible boats and high-explosive warheads – it will be such a war as has never been seen!'

He sat, gazing into his glass for a while, then raised his eyes to his brother.

'Sherlock,' he said, 'you were, I believe, upset when King Edward stopped your pursuit of the astronomer . . .'

'Nonsense,' said Holmes. 'I did not share his view of the danger, but he asked when he might have commanded and I felt obliged to bow to his wishes.'

'Would it interest you to know that, in his last hours, King Edward sent me a message for you?'

'A message?' said Holmes.

'Yes. Even in your rural retreat you must have heard the gossip that the King's friend Mrs Keppel was brought to his

114

death-bed, by permission of the Queen? Between us here, that is true, and it was Mrs Keppel who conveyed the King's message. She, poor lady, thought His Majesty was wandering in his mind when he told her, "Tell Mycroft that his brother should resume the hunt"!'

Holmes' dark eyes lit. 'So he maintained his responsibilities to the last! Is his successor privy to our story?'

'No, Sherlock. He will not take so direct a part in international policy as his father. It is better that he knows nothing.'

'Very well. You told me, some time since, that you had smelt out the rat in your office, Mycroft. Is he still in place?'

'Oh, indeed. He has been extremely useful to me as a way of feeding false information to the All Highest.'

'I fear that it is time to end his career. I must examine him tomorrow morning.'

The following morning Holmes and I waited on Mycroft at his office. He sat behind his large desk, a single manilla folder on his blotter, when we were shown in. Without a word he passed it across to his brother. Holmes skimmed through it rapidly, giving me a quick summary of its contents as he did so.

'Howard Hugo, aged twenty-one, only son of respectable tradespeople in Peckham, entered the Service by examination four years ago, a Registry clerk, polite and industrious according to his superiors, no disciplinary matters.'

He replaced the file on the desk. 'What brought him to your attention, Mycroft?'

'He was one of the few who knew of our arrangements to send Miss Norton on the Bristol train from Glasgow, and among the very few who did not know that the arrangement had been changed. In a Department of State all information eventually passes through the Registry for recording and filing, but that change was made so late that the information did not reach the Registry in time to be betrayed. That placed him and a few colleagues under my suspicion. A close watch was kept on him, which revealed that he had periods of financial embarrassment when he borrowed small sums from colleagues, followed by periods when he was inexplicably flush. That, essentially, is my case.'

'Where is he now?' asked Holmes.

'He is at work in the Registry. I thought it better that you should question him – he may confess the more readily under the weight of your reputation.'

'Then send for him, my dear brother, and let us have this thing out.'

Mycroft pressed the button on his desk and after a few moments there was a tap at the door. At Mycroft's command the door opened to admit a youth of middle height clad in the discreet garb of a junior clerk.

'Sit down, Hugo,' said Mycroft as the boy approached his desk. 'These gentlemen wish to put some questions to you. They are Mr Sherlock Holmes and his colleague, Dr Watson. I am sure you will have heard of them.'

Hugo slumped, rather than sat, in an empty chair and his hands flew together in his lap. His complexion was already pale, but now all colour was completely drained from his face. He looked from Holmes to his brother and back again.

'Is there some question of my work, sir?' he stammered.

'Oh, indeed,' said Holmes. 'A serious question as to who you have been working for!'

'I don't believe I understand you . . .' began the boy, but Holmes sprang towards him and dragged him bodily from the chair. His hands flew over the youth's jacket as fast as a conjuror's and he flung two objects on to Mycroft's desk before dropping the terrified young man back into his chair.

'Let me make one thing clear, Mr Hugo,' said Holmes, resuming his seat. 'I am not here to be trifled with. You are a junior clerk, earning, at most, a few pounds a month, yet the slight smear of ash on your right sleeve betokens a taste for cigars – the green-leaved Indian variety. They are an unduly expensive taste for a person in your situation.'

He paused and picked something from the table. 'Here is your watch,' he said, flicking open the case with his thumb-nail and turning it to the light. 'The pawnbrokers' pin-marks on the inside of the case confirm what I already knew, that your financial affairs fluctuate alarmingly. That might be women, drink or horses, but in your case it is cards. Is this not a box of cards?' and he pointed to a small box on the desk.

Hugo was in tears before Holmes had done.

'I'm sorry, sir,' he sobbed to Mycroft. 'I got into playing cards and plunged too heavily. I hope I have not dishonoured the department!'

'If you have dishonoured my office,' said Mycroft, and his face was very grave, 'it is not in a taste for Indian cigars nor in unwise gambling. You know, I think, that it is much more serious than that!'

'Oh, heavens!' cried the luckless young man. 'You know it all!' and a fresh paroxysm of weeping shook him.

'Now, Mr Hugo,' said Sherlock Holmes, 'you must tell us all of the truth. To whom have you been selling the secrets of your department?'

'I went to a public house one night – with my cousin Jack, he's a sailor. He took me to it, said it was the place for a good night's fun.'

'Where was it?' asked Holmes, as the boy paused.

'It was by the West India Docks, the Railway Tavern.'

Holmes laughed mirthlessly. 'More often known as Charlie Brown's – I know it. Carry on with your tale.'

'Well, we got in a game of cards and I won some money – not a lot, just a few shillings.'

'How long was it before you started losing, Mr Hugo?'

'I went back several times and I kept winning for about two weeks. Then I had a run of bad luck. I kept losing every time. I lost more than I could afford. That was when I pawned my watch the first time. Then one night I lost to a sailor and I couldn't pay. I didn't know what to do. He threatened me with a knife. He was very drunk and I thought he would kill me.'

'But then someone paid your debt,' said Holmes. 'Who was he? Who paid the debt?'

'I don't remember seeing him there before. He was an ordinary sort of man, a Londoner, he said his name was Baker. He said I could repay him any time, but I kept on losing.'

'And then he said you could do him a favour in return for the loan and so you began to give him information about the work of this department!' finished Holmes.

'Yes sir, but he said there was no harm in it – he said he was a reporter for a news agency, that was all. After the first time he started paying me for things I told him.'

'Tell me more about this Mr Baker?' said Holmes. 'What was he like?'

'He was about as big as Dr Watson here, but plump – no, fat. He had a moustache . . .'

'What colour?' asked Holmes. 'How did he speak?'

'His moustache was very fair, sir, and his hair. He spoke like a Londoner, sir – south or east of the City, I should say, from his accent.'

'Did you always meet him at Charlie Brown's? Do you know where he lived?' asked Holmes.

'It was always at Charlie Brown's, sir. I saw him a dozen times, I suppose. I never knew where he lived, but he came with a sailor one night and I heard the sailor say something about them getting back to Deptford, but I don't know if he lives there.'

'Whatever else he is, Mr Baker is almost certainly not an agency reporter,' said Holmes. 'What do you imagine he does for a living? How did he dress?'

'He said he was a reporter, sir, but he might have been a small tradesman or something like that. He dressed respectably, not showy or flash, just respectably.'

Sherlock Holmes rose. 'I think', he said to Mycroft, 'that is all Mr Hugo can usefully tell us. Whatever disposal is made of him, he should not be allowed any contact with anyone who is not watched.'

'I shall arrange it,' said Mycroft. He picked up his telephone and gave a few words of instruction. The door opened, seconds later, to admit two large young men with the look of ex-soldiers.

'You know where to take Mr Hugo,' Mycroft told them, and they took hold of the young man by an elbow each.

As they propelled him towards the door the youth turned his white face to Holmes. 'Will they hang me, Mr Holmes?' he asked, almost in a whisper.

'Since we are not at war, no,' said Holmes, 'but I think you will have a long time to reflect on your stupidity, cowardice and treachery.'

Mycroft Holmes gazed long at the door when it had closed behind the trio. 'I cannot recollect this ever happening before,' he said, 'in any department – let alone my own!'

'What will be done with him?' asked Holmes. 'There must not be a trial, lest we alarm Mr Baker.'

118

'The department has a house near Epsom – its neighbours believe it to be a clinic for the morally deranged – where Mr Hugo may reflect on his behaviour for as long as is necessary. It has high walls and a number of young men such as the two you have just seen,' said Mycroft.

'Good!' said Holmes. 'We have at least learned something more of the operations of German Intelligence. I must apply my enquiries more closely in the Deptford area, to see if I can uncover this Mr Baker.'

'But he does not sound like the astronomer!' I said.

'No, but he was the conduit through which information sold by that witless little traitor reached the astronomer and may lead me to him.'

As we left, Holmes turned back to his brother. 'From now on,' he said, 'you must be very careful. Hugo's disappearance will show them that you know of his treachery, and you no longer have King Edward's protection.'

'Are you suggesting that they will seek to assassinate me?' asked Mycroft.

'It was you, dear brother, who warned us years ago that we were playing against the most cunning and ruthless of the Kaiser's agents,' said Holmes. 'I repeat: be very careful!'

AN OUTRAGE AT THE DIOGENES CLUB

Holmes sought his man at Charlie Brown's, but he was not to be found. It seemed that the disappearance of young Hugo had made the German agent take fright. Disguised as all manner of seafarers from a variety of places, Holmes haunted the dockside taverns, but without success.

During this exercise he made my home his headquarters, returning from his wanderings in Limehouse to scribble pages of his book on bee-keeping. One evening in early autumn he was deep in a bundle of manuscript while I leafed through a magazine, when we heard the voice of a newsboy crying a headline.

Holmes flung open the window and leaned out to hear more clearly. I got up and joined him. 'Listen, Watson!' he said. 'He is crying a Special Edition. There has been a bomb in Pall Mall! We must go there at once!'

I sent my boy to fetch a newspaper and summon a cab. As we set out for Pall Mall, Holmes spread the paper across his knees. The still-wet headlines proclaimed: ANARCHIST OUTRAGE AT A GENTLEMEN'S CLUB. TERROR IN THE HEART OF OUR CAPITAL.

The newspaper had gone to press so rapidly that few details were revealed, only that the Diogenes Club had been attacked with an explosive device earlier that evening and a number of its members killed. Holmes's face grew pale and grim as he thrust the sheets into my hand.

In Pall Mall a police officer ordered our cabbie to stop. Holmes explained that he was a club member's brother and the officer assisted us through the crowd of onlookers that stood deeply around the front of the building.

Once through the crowd we could see that the police had roped off a space in front of the club, where two fire engines stood. The outside of the building seemed hardly to have suffered, but the steps and lobby were littered with broken glass, splinters and smashed wood, where the handsome glazed doors had been blown outwards. From the interior black smoke still drifted as firemen and policemen went about their business.

Holmes strode up to a police inspector who seemed to be in charge.

'I am Sherlock Holmes,' he said. 'Can you tell me, Inspector, if everyone has been got out of the building?'

'Why, Mr Holmes!' said the inspector. 'Yes, sir, they've all been got out, living and dead. Was there someone you wanted to know about?'

'My brother is a member,' said Holmes. 'A man of my height, but more portly.'

The inspector consulted his notebook. 'Would that be Mr Mycroft Holmes, sir? He was all right, sir. In fact he was helping with the rescue until they was all out, then he went off home.'

'Thank you, Inspector,' said Holmes, and, pushing his way through the crowd, he swung away briskly across the street.

Mycroft's elderly valet, looking deeply disturbed, admitted us to the apartment.

'How is he, Mortimer?' demanded Holmes.

'He is unharmed, sir, I believe, but it's a dreadful business, Mr Sherlock. Mr Mycroft has only been home a few minutes, sir. He's extremely upset and angry, sir.'

He showed us into the library, where Holmes paced up and down impatiently, pulling books out and replacing them until Mycroft joined us. The elder Holmes' face, normally pale, was chalk-white, and dressings covered two small injuries to his right cheek and temple. Nevertheless he managed a bantering tone.

'Sherlock!' he cried. 'You have rushed all the way from Sussex, and brought me medical attention too!'

'I am in no mood for jokes, Mycroft,' snapped Holmes, 'and nor should you be! This is exactly what I warned you against!'

Mycroft lowered himself carefully into a large leather armchair and rang for Mortimer. When drinks had been poured he smiled at us wanly over his glass.

'You have every right to be angry, Sherlock. I was remiss in discounting your fears for my safety. Now, alas, five of my fellow members have paid for my carelessness.'

'What happened?' asked Holmes.

'I had not long arrived at the club and was taking a drink in the reading room, just off the lobby, when the porter brought me a message that there was a foreign gentleman in the lobby who would not give a name but desired to see me most urgently. I turned to see if I could spy the stranger through the glass doors, and that was what saved my life.'

'How was that?' asked Holmes.

'Evidently the scoundrel knew my habit of taking a drink in the reading room on my arrival, and relied on the porter coming to me to confirm my identity to him. He had stepped up to the door and pushed it ajar. Just as I turned to look for him, he rolled something across the floor towards me. I saw at once that it was black and spherical and had a burning fuse attached.'

He paused and refilled his glass.

'I took it to be an explosive device,' he said. 'I had time only to shout one word of warning and to make shift to protect myself and the porter. I took the poor old fellow and flung him across my chair, at the same time throwing myself and the chair over to the left. My fellow members, I'm sorry to say, did not respond so quickly. Most of them were still muttering at my breach of the rules when the wretched thing exploded.'

'What did it do?' demanded Holmes.

'It went off with a roar like a dozen cannon. The windows blew out and there was shrapnel hurled all around us, but the back and base of the chair saved the porter and me from the worst of it. When I got up, the room was a shambles. It was full of stinking smoke, the carpet was ablaze in several places and the whole place was littered with broken furniture and fellows who'd been caught in the blast.'

'Whereupon,' said Holmes sternly, 'you continued to expose yourself to danger by assisting in the rescue! Will you now take warning, Mycroft?'

'I concede again that I have ignored the warning I urged upon you, Sherlock, but what am I to do? I cannot live behind iron gates until such time as the Emperor of Germany forgets me!'

'Firstly,' said Holmes, 'you might withdraw a couple of those hard-faced young men from your department's house at Epsom, and deploy them as your personal bodyguards.'

'Really, Sherlock!' said Mycroft. 'I cannot go about my affairs attended by two bodyguards as though I were some prize-fight promoter!'

'If you have no care for your person,' snapped Holmes, 'consider the importance of the office you hold and the safety of the country that employs you!'

'Very well,' replied Mycroft, chastened by his brother's outburst. 'What next?'

'You must continue to allow the newspapers to treat this as an anarchist outrage. They believe so at present and it should be no difficulty for your office to feed them misleading information.'

'You and I know very well whence this attack has come, Sherlock. Why should we pretend otherwise?'

'To facilitate my investigations into the real origin of the attack and to convince our enemies that we are pursuing a false trail. Finally, you must have a friendly word with your colleagues at the Russian Embassy – I need the name of their most able agent among the Russian immigrants in the East End.'

'Even if they are willing to supply that information, it is bound to cost my department some concession that we are desperately anxious to avoid,' said Mycroft. 'Why do you need it?'

'Because the Czar's secret police have been active in the East End ever since his disillusioned subjects began fleeing here from his beneficent rule. They will know more of the secrets of the political gangs in the East End than any London policeman or your own office.'

'Very well,' said Mycroft reluctantly. 'Now, if you will excuse me, this evening's events have shaken me a little and I propose to turn in.'

As we made our way back down Pall Mall I noticed a thin smile playing over my friend's lips and asked the reason.

'It occurs to me, Watson, that the Diogenes Club will never be the same now that my brother has shouted in the reading room. I wonder if his fellow members will blackball him!'

Shaken he may well have been, but Mycroft was as good as his word. Late next morning a messenger from his office brought a brief note:

My dear Sherlock,
The Warsaw Restaurant is a Jewish establishment in Osborne Street, off the Whitechapel Road.

The proprietor is one Alexander Snelwar. Put on one of your most impenetrable disguises and tell Snelwar that Hymie sent you to change a large cheque.

Ask him to introduce you to 'The Landlord', who is always there after two.

Your affectionate brother, M.

19

ADVENTURES AMONG THE ANARCHISTS

The account that I must give of Sherlock Holmes' exploits in the East End derives, inevitably, from his own telling. Lacking his facility in disguise and dialects I could not join him among the European *émigrés* who frequented the Warsaw Restaurant.

Within an hour of Mycroft's message I found myself host to an elderly, bespectacled street musician, clad in a long, threadbare overcoat to which his mittened fingers clutched a battered fiddle wrapped in chamois. In a thick accent, reminiscent of Middle Europe, he bade me farewell and slipped out of my side door.

At Osborne Street the Warsaw Restaurant was crowded, its windows dull with grime and steam. Inside, the workless of Whitechapel played cards or chess, talked loudly in half a dozen languages, or simply dawdled over a cup of black tea to avoid facing the autumn streets of the East End. The atmosphere in the eating-house was stiflingly warm and thick with coarse tobacco smoke, underlaid with the sharp odour of cabbage.

Holmes threaded his way to the counter and ordered a black tea. When he was served he asked, 'Are you Snelwar?'

The proprietor grunted. 'Who vants to know?' he demanded.

'Hymie said you know a man who would change a big cheque for me. "The Landlord", is it?'

'Over there,' said Snelwar, jerking his head towards a corner of the room where a single customer sat in a corner well away from the gas brackets. 'There is the one we call The Landlord.'

Holmes thanked him and picked his way carefully through the room, clutching his fiddle in one hand and his tea in the other. At the corner table he set down his tea then laid his violin carefully on an empty chair before seating himself opposite The Landlord.

He sipped his tea and drew a noisy breath of appreciation while he sized up the man opposite. The Landlord was a small man, in middle age. He wore a black suit that had seen better days. Above his neatly trimmed, greying beard and waxed moustache a pair of bright, black eyes watched Holmes from a swarthy, oval face.

'Are you this Landlord man?' asked Holmes.

'I am Leon Beron,' said his companion. 'In here they call me The Landlord, yes.'

'Hymie said you would change a large cheque for me. Is that so?'

'You are the British agent,' stated Beron, without changing his tone. 'What do you know of me?'

'That you are Russian by birth, but you have lived in France and in London for some years,' said Holmes.

'And who tells you this?' asked Beron sharply.

'Your voice tells me this,' said Holmes, 'and the fact that I have been sent to you tells me that you are the best Russian agent in London.'

'Why are you sent?' said Beron. 'What do you want?'

'I want a man,' said Holmes, 'a German spy.'

'Why should I help you?' asked Beron.

'Because your Government has told you to, because this man is an enemy of both our countries,' said Holmes, and sipped his tea.

'My Government, as you are pleased to call it, expects me to watch over my fellow countrymen – those hotheads who plan the downfall of the Czar – not to chase German spies for you, Mr Holmes!'

'*Touché*!' said Holmes. 'May I ask how you know me?'

'Your policemen come in here, disguised as tramps and sailors, even the agents of your brother's department, but we see them and we know them. You are very good, Mr Holmes. You fooled Snelwar, who is very careful. Who else would you be but Mycroft Holmes' famous brother?'

'Does Snelwar protect you, then?'

Beron laughed. 'There are a dozen people in this room who would murder me if they knew my real business. Snelwar and

126

his friends think I am a moneylender and changer, and so I am. I sit here every day from two to midnight and they bring me their cheques from home and I change them. While I change them I talk to them and I learn their dreams and their plans. So, for very little effort, I keep my masters happy by selling these people to them.'

'You do not seem to take any pleasure in your work,' remarked Holmes.

Beron looked at him steadily, then picked up his teacup. 'The reasons why I do what I do are between me and my Government, Mr Holmes. They have some methods of persuasion of which you may have heard.'

'All your intelligence is gathered here, in this little restaurant?' asked Holmes.

'No, Mr Holmes, it is gathered all over London by people who are my eyes and ears. Some of them know what they do and do it for small sums of money, some do it out of political spite, and some do it unknowingly because they cannot help boasting about themselves and their friends. For example – you see the group to your left, with the cards?'

Holmes had already observed them and nodded.

'The man in the middle, with the fierce moustaches, he interests my Government. Here he calls himself Peter Piatkow or Peter Straume, but his name is really Gederts Eliass. He steals money to buy arms for revolution in Russia. Now he and his friends are not just playing cards. They are planning to rob a jeweller in Houndsditch.'

'What will you do?' asked Holmes.

'Do, Mr Holmes? Nothing! I shall tell my masters and go on sitting here. If they want to know where the money goes they will let the robbery go ahead. If they want to embarrass your Government they will tell your policemen and when the robbers are caught there will be loud cries from your newspapers to stop immigration. Either way, I shall still sit here.'

The little man sipped his tea again. 'Now,' he said, 'tell me about your German spy.'

Holmes told him all that he knew of 'Mr Baker', while Beron nodded thoughtfully. When Holmes had done, Beron asked, 'And what is it that you want?'

'I want to know where he is, without him knowing that I seek him. I want to know about his associates, particularly if they include a well-spoken, bearded Englishman who also speaks Spanish.'

'You do not want much!' laughed Beron. 'Now, finish your tea and go. Come back one week today – not like the fiddler, like someone else. I may have news for you by then.'

Holmes returned to Sussex, but a week later my door bell sounded as I sat in my study one evening. The boy announced that a bookseller had called with some volumes for me to see and was waiting in the drawing-room.

Entering the drawing-room I saw a bent old man in tinted spectacles laying out a number of pamphlets on the table. He straightened as I came in.

'Dr Watson?' he asked. 'The celebrated Dr Watson, Mr Holmes' colleague?' His voice was rasping and bronchitic.

'I have that honour, yes,' I replied. 'What have you brought me?'

'Here', he wheezed, 'is a complete set of "God's Vengeance Upon Murder Discovered", only a little mildewed. Even the British Museum hasn't got a set!'

I stepped to the table and examined the booklets under the lamp. A familiar voice spoke behind me.

'I am glad to hear you describe our association as an honour, Watson!'

I spun round to find Holmes behind me, pulling off the seedy overcoat of the bookseller and throwing off his wig and spectacles. 'Holmes!' I cried. 'You always deceive me with your disguises!'

He laughed and dropped into an armchair. 'I have been meeting with Beron. Now, do you think I might have some coffee? That dark brew they serve at the Warsaw Restaurant has ruined my taste for tea.'

While he drank his coffee he described his meeting with Beron. Holmes had joined him at his usual table in the Warsaw Restaurant, saying that the old musician had sent him.

Beron smiled. 'Really,' he said, 'your repertoire is remarkable. I could use a man with such talents!'

Holmes smiled in return. 'I regret that I cannot accept your offer, Beron. Even if I were not retired I do not believe my brother would wish me to involve myself in the Czar's affairs.'

'A pity!' said Beron, and shrugged. 'However, I have some news of your Mr Baker.'

'Splendid!' said Holmes. 'You have tracked him down?'

'Not yet to his home,' said Beron, 'but one of my friends knows where he can be found.'

He turned and signalled to a dark man seated at another table, who rose and came over to them. He was a lean, dramatically handsome young man and, above his high cheekbones, his dark eyes burned in a pale face.

'This is Morry,' said Beron. 'Sit down, Morry, and tell this gentleman about the man you have been looking for.'

The young man slid into a seat, sitting nervously upright. 'Who is this, Beron?' he asked, indicating Holmes.

'All you need to know, Morry, is that I know who he is and where he comes from. He does not ask all about you!'

'No,' said Holmes. 'Apart from the fact that you have lived in Australia and have been recently in prison, I know nothing of you.'

Morry recoiled and started from his seat. 'Who is he?' he demanded of Beron. 'How does he know about me?'

'Sit down!' said Beron. 'I vouch for this man, but perhaps I should have warned you that there are very sharp eyes behind those spectacles.'

'I did not mean to disturb you,' said Holmes. 'I merely observed your hair and the pallor of your face. Also, while your English is almost Cockney, you draw some words out like an Australian. You have been seeking Mr Baker for me?'

'I have found Mr Baker for you,' said the young man. 'He is back among the sailors' pubs by St Katherine's. Once or twice a week you will see him in one or another.'

'What does he do there?' asked Holmes.

'He talks with foreign sailors, drinks with them, plays cards with them. And I tell you something else – I know what his trade is.'

'Really?' said Holmes. 'And what is that?'

'He is a baker,' said Morry. 'He calls himself after his work!'

'How do you know this?' asked Holmes.

'In a bakery you sweat all the time – I know, I have worked in them. Flour sticks to your eyebrows and your hair. I have seen it on him. He is a baker.'

129

'Excellent work!' said Holmes. 'May we expect to know soon where he keeps his ovens?'

'Very soon, if I know Morry,' said Beron, 'but you should not come here again. Tell me where to send messages and you shall hear any news as soon as I do.'

Holmes gave them my address, impressing upon them that no one must ever call there, then left with his mildewed pamphlets.

Holly appeared in florists' windows as Christmas approached, and the pavements of Ludgate Hill were thronged with sellers of German clockwork toys. It was some three weeks before the holiday when we learned from the newspapers that Beron had been right in at least one thing. A group of foreign anarchists had been surprised in the East End, trying to tunnel into a jeweller's on Houndsditch. Shots had been fired and, after a running battle in the streets, three constables were dead. The perpetrators had vanished into the slums.

The press was loud in its condemnation of the outrage and, as Beron had predicted, demanded laws against immigration. For some time the police seemed to have no idea of the whereabouts of the anarchists.

In the early twilight of Christmas Eve Holmes and I were sitting either side of the fire in my study when we heard the shuffle of feet and the subdued voices of children at my front door.

'Carol singers,' I remarked, and made my way to the door to listen to them. I was confronted by a quintet of ragamuffins, wrapped in the warmest tatters they could muster. At my appearance they burst into an ill-rehearsed performance of "God Rest You Merry, Gentlemen", sung in the unmistakable accents of Stepney and Whitechapel.

At the finale the tallest of the band stepped forward and wished me 'A merry Christmas an' a 'appy New Year, guvnor!' while his choir waited expectantly. Their pinched faces brightened as I felt in my pocket for change and dropped it into the leader's hand. They were off in a moment, with cries of 'Ta, guvnor!', their boots clattering away into the dusk, and, as they disappeared, I realised that the boy had cunningly passed me a folded paper while receiving my donation.

I unfolded it under the gas lamp in the hall, and when I had seen its contents, took it at once to Holmes. It was a message from Beron and said:

The money-changer sends the bookseller and the fiddler Christmas greetings and a gift – the baker is Peter Hahn of 201 High Street, Deptford.

MURDER ON CLAPHAM COMMON

I had imagined that Beron's information might send Holmes to spend the holiday in disguise in Deptford, but he reminded me that the baker would be busy with his legitimate Christmas trade and his illicit contacts would have to wait. So it was that we were still together on New Year's Eve, and shared a bottle in the last hour of the Old Year, lifting a glass to young 1911 and hoping for a peaceful and prosperous New Year.

That we were not to be at peace long, we discovered soon enough, for the newspapers of 2nd January informed us that a man had been found murdered on Clapham Common at dawn on New Year's Day – and that man was Leon Beron!

A policeman had discovered the body where it had been dragged under some bushes. Beron had been struck down and stabbed on an asphalt path nearby. The police believed he was slain at about three in the morning, having been beaten about the head with an instrument like a crowbar or a thieves' jemmy. His watch and chain, with a gold five-pound piece, were missing, as was a wash-leather purse which he kept filled with sovereigns and pinned inside his waistcoat pocket, and the police seemed to believe that robbery was the motive.

'What do you make of it, Holmes?' I asked, when he had digested the reports.

'This is not robbery, Watson,' said Holmes. 'Beron almost certainly informed the police of the Houndsditch robbery, and he identified Peter Hahn for me. Now he is found dead, apparently at the hands of casual thieves. Coincidence, Watson, is the willing servant of the lazy mind. No – poor Beron was not murdered for a few sovereigns, but because he was a spy. The knife wounds prove it!'

'The knife wounds?' I asked.

'He was killed by blows to the head, but there were stab wounds to the body as well, and knife marks on his face. On each cheek the letter S was cut with a knife-point. What does that signify?'

'I have no idea!'

'I venture to suggest that it is the initial of the word "spy", or perhaps its Russian equivalent – "*spic*". Indeed, the repeated letter on each cheek may indicate "Secret Service".'

'You mean he was killed for passing information to the police – or to you?' I asked.

'One or the other, Watson. Someone lured him to Clapham Common. Why did he go there? He was as fixed in his habits as Mycroft, or even more so. Mycroft has three points in his orbit. Beron had but two – his lodgings and the Warsaw Restaurant. Who drew him to Clapham Common in the dead of night, and on what pretext?'

Holmes mulled over the newspapers all afternoon, but announced no further conclusions. It was well after dark when there came a clamorous ringing at my bell. My housekeeper appeared in a state of confusion.

'There's a gentleman in the hall, doctor, who says he wants to talk to the bookseller with the blue spectacles! I told him there's no bookseller here, but he's most insistent!'

Holmes laughed. 'Show him in, Louisa,' he said.

She had barely turned back to the door when it swung open to reveal a young man with piercing black eyes. He was smartly dressed but dishevelled, and he was evidently under some great strain. He strode into the room, his eyes swivelling about him nervously. He stopped short at the sight of Holmes and me, and a look of bewilderment crossed his face.

'Where is the old bookseller?' he demanded.

'I am the bookseller,' said Holmes, and the bronchitic rasp entered his voice. 'Have a chair, Morry, and tell us what brings you here.'

Morry dropped into a chair, staring at Holmes. 'You are the bookseller?' he exclaimed, and peered closer. 'Yes, you are! Beron was right – he said you were the cleverest man in London!'

'An exaggeration, I think,' said Holmes, in his normal tones.

'I am merely painstaking in certain small ways. But you did not come here to discuss my reputation – you came because of Beron's death.'

'Who are you?' asked Morry suspiciously.

'I am Sherlock Holmes and this is my friend and colleague, Dr Watson. Now it is only fair that you tell us who you really are!'

'Sherlock Holmes!' exclaimed the young man. 'I am – I am Morris Stein. They also call me Steinie Morrison. You must help me, Mr Holmes!'

'We shall see,' said Holmes. 'Why do you need my help?'

'They say I killed Beron! They say I took him to Clapham and beat him to death!'

'And did you?' asked Holmes.

'No, Mr Holmes, I swear it! Beron was my friend. He paid me money, he gave me work. Why would I kill him?'

'Then why do they say you killed him?'

'I was at the Warsaw Restaurant with him on New Year's Eve. We ate, we talked, then I went. Now people say I came back, that we went out together at midnight. I didn't, Mr Holmes. I went to – I went to see a young lady.'

'I understand that Beron rarely left the restaurant in normal circumstances?' said Holmes.

'That is right,' said Morrison. 'He wouldn't have gone anywhere unless it was very important, especially not so late.'

'It must have been someone whom he trusted – as he trusted you, Mr Morrison!'

'It wasn't me, Mr Holmes! I think someone lied to draw him to Clapham.'

'Why would they do that?' asked Holmes.

'Everyone in the Warsaw Restaurant wants to know who set the police on the anarchists. Beron lived right next door to their club. They killed him because they think he spied on them and they've got me blamed because I worked for him!'

'That makes sense, I grant you,' said Holmes, 'but why should I help you?'

'Because I didn't kill him, Mr Holmes!' said Morrison, and paused.

Holmes made no reply and after a moment the young man added, 'And because I can do something for you!'

'Ha!' exclaimed Holmes. 'What is that?'

'I can tell you where Peter Hahn sends his information and where he gets his orders from!'

Holmes' eyes glittered. 'Let me be quite straight with you, Morrison,' he said. 'I did not know if you killed Beron when you first came here, but I had already formed the view that he was killed for passing information. There is no reason for you to have done that. For you to murder Beron and mark his corpse to brand him as a spy would be arrant foolishness, since it would draw attention to your dealings with him. Nevertheless, you might have been one of his killers. If I help you it will be because I believe you innocent, not because of anything you can tell me about Peter Hahn.'

'Why do you think him innocent?' I interjected.

'Because he might have come here tonight and told me he would trade information if I would help him, but he did not do so straight away. He told me I should help him because he is innocent.'

He turned back to Morrison. 'I cannot guarantee that I can help you escape the trap that has been set for you, but I will do my utmost.'

'I cannot ask for more, Mr Holmes.'

'Now tell me what you know of Peter Hahn.'

'I got to work for him, working casual on his Christmas orders. Soon I could see it was no ordinary bakery. He got letters every day – from all over the place.'

'What manner of letters?' asked Holmes.

'The envelopes were mostly handwritten, some of them by foreigners – many had the figure 1 in the address with a tail, as they write it on the Continent, and sometimes there were words misspelled.'

'Where were they from?' asked Holmes.

'All over England,' said Morrison, 'and from abroad, sometimes – Amsterdam, Dublin, New York, I remember.'

'Do you have any idea what was in them?'

'I used to see that Hahn never sent replies, but he wrote only one letter each day. Sometimes I would offer to post it, but he always took it himself. One night when he had gone to bed and left us working in the bakery, I looked in his office.'

'What did you find?'

'That morning's letters, Mr Holmes – reports from German agents all over the country, and a copy-book!'

'A copy-book!' exclaimed Holmes. 'He cannot have been so stupid!'

'They are very methodical, these Germans, they keep records of everything. His copy-book had copies of his reports to his master. I had not much time but I saw who those reports went to,' and he handed Holmes a slip of paper from his pocket.

Holmes read the paper and his eyes flashed. 'This is excellent!' he cried. 'You have done very well indeed, and in return I shall do whatever lies in my power for you.'

He sent Morrison away with instructions to lie low, and the following morning we visited Mycroft's office. To our amazement he was not there, but by the time we met him in the rebuilt Strangers' Room at the Diogenes Club that night we had seen the newspapers.

The anarchist murder gang had been found by police in a boarding house in Sidney Street, Stepney, and surrounded. At first light they had opened fire on the police and a decision had been taken to call in the Army. Surrounded by seven hundred soldiers, the anarchists had maintained their defiance, even when a Maxim gun was brought against them.

The Home Secretary, Mr Winston Churchill, had attended in person and, when the house caught fire, had ordered the fire brigade to stand back and let it burn.

The bodies of two anarchists had been found in the ruins, but neither was Eliass, or 'Peter the Painter' as the newspapers called him. The police, apparently, did not know his real name, for when a reward of five hundred pounds was offered for him it was under the name of 'Peter Piatkow'. It produced no result and he remains at large.

This extraordinary episode in the heart of London set the public agog, and drew more attention to the murder of Beron. Morrison was now publicly identified as the last person seen in Beron's company.

Holmes greeted his brother with a smile. 'You have been in the East End then, dear brother?' he asked.

Mycroft was not amused. 'If Cabinet Ministers have no more sense than to expose themselves to assassins' guns, I do not see why the Civil Service should take the same foolhardy risks. Yes,

I have been in the East End, and now you have come to tell me that the man Morrison did not murder Leon Beron.'

Holmes raised his eyebrows. 'I see that danger does not interfere with your rational function,' he remarked. 'That is exactly why I am here.'

'Why do you imagine that I can do anything about it?' asked Mycroft, plying his snuffbox.

'I had not imagined that the question was whether you could, Mycroft, but whether you would. Even the newspaper reports make it clear that he is the victim of a political conspiracy.'

'But that conspiracy will have ended. Two of the anarchists' leaders are dead and the small fry are being hunted through the East End. They have other matters to concern them than the fate of Steinie Morrison.'

'That would be so if Morrison's enemies were the anarchists,' said Holmes, 'but if, as I believe, Beron died for trafficking with me, then Morrison is still in deadly danger.'

Mycroft looked thoughtful. 'This is difficult, brother,' he said. 'The public knows of the hunt for Morrison. Scotland Yard has witnesses who place them together all the way to Clapham Common, and today's events have fanned the outcry against the political gangs. This department manages miracles all the time, but I fear I cannot prevent Morrison's arrest and trial!'

'Tut, Mycroft!' said Holmes. 'It is not arrest and trial he objects to so very strongly – it is being hanged at the end of it! Now, I'm sure you can prevent that!'

'I shall have to consider the matter very carefully,' said Mycroft. 'You will have to give me time.'

What agreement was struck between the brothers I never knew, for I was not present at their next meeting. I know that, after it, Holmes sent word to Morrison to come out of hiding. A week after New Year he was arrested while breakfasting in an East End café and charged with the murder of Beron.

The committal proceedings against him were extraordinary. There were plenty of witnesses to say that he and Beron had left the Warsaw Restaurant in company, that Morrison had carried a weighty parcel and that they were seen in the streets together. There were cabmen who said they had taken both to Clapham Common and brought only Morrison back. There was a girl who saw Morrison with Beron's gold piece after the crime and a youth who saw Morrison with a pistol, though both of these withdrew their evidence. After the magistrates' court proceedings, a cabman (who had already changed his evidence once) was attacked by three ruffians who received sentences of hard labour, though no one seemed to know on whose behalf they were tampering with the witness.

The trial in March ended with Steinie's conviction and the inevitable death sentence. An appeal was rejected, but in such terms that, on 12th April, the Home Secretary commuted Morrison's sentence to imprisonment for life. Holmes smiled when he read of it in the paper.

'I do not know why you smile, Holmes,' I remarked. 'You said that you believed Morrison innocent. Now the poor wretch has gone to life imprisonment.'

'My dear Watson,' said Holmes. 'The public, which clamours and crowds into the Old Bailey to watch a sensational murder trial, and waits all night to see the hanging certificate posted, loses all interest in a man who is sentenced to life imprisonment. Where Steinie Morrison may be is, as from today, a matter of complete obscurity.'

I did not understand his reply at the time, nor for some years after, but some inkling of the explanation was given me by a recent chance meeting with Athelney Jones. He accosted me in a public house and, over a glass, told me that he is now attached to the Counter-Espionage Division of the Ministry of Munitions, a matter which I imagine he should not have been discussing in a public house, if at all. Knowing nothing of Holmes' connection with the Clapham case, he dropped a hint that, so far from serving a sentence of life imprisonment, Morrison was somewhere in the North of England investigating a plot against the Prime Minister!

THE MAKING OF ALTAMONT

Whatever the truth of Morrison's life sentence, once it was announced Holmes returned to Sussex, saying only that Morrison's information would help him eliminate further suspects. As always I awaited news of his activities and, as always, received little. From occasional notes I learned that Mr Kelly of Willesden was short and fat, and that Dr Barton had been in Belgium at the time of the railway disasters. The gentleman in the West Riding was not a Spanish speaker, but married to a Spanish wife. Of our two South Americans, Mr Pereira's appearance confirmed Holmes' predictions, but for a long time he could get no information about Alvarez.

The late summer of 1911 saw Holmes' book on bees safe in the hands of the printer, and he disappeared beyond my ken for a few months, as he continued to travel the country seeking out his suspects. The Kaiser stirred himself that summer and tried to provoke a crisis in Morocco. The newspapers talked of war and I know now that, in late August, the Imperial Defence Committee began to prepare a strategy for war.

In late autumn a note from Holmes told me that he would be at Fulworth for Christmas and invited me to join him.

Christmas passed without interruption and on Boxing Day we were so heavy from Martha's table and Holmes' cellar that I insisted we should wrap ourselves warmly and take a little exercise. We strolled in a leisurely fashion up the slope of the downs behind Holmes' villa, where an ancient trackway climbed through the trees and over the hill's crest. The bare branches were black against a luminous winter sky and beech-mast crackled underfoot as Holmes recited more details of his suspects.

'I solved one small mystery, Watson,' he told me, 'when I called at Miss Morgan's Practical Crafts Shop in Aldgate.'

'Surely she is not the astronomer!' I joked.

'No, Watson,' said Holmes, with a dry chuckle, 'but she is the mistress of a certain missing husband from Tunbridge Wells. I hope that his wife has resigned herself to his absence after so long. I would not wish to be the one that tells her that he now lives in unwedded bliss with a socialist schoolteacher!'

We laughed and he continued. 'I have eliminated some others. I have met with the writer of songs, and he is not our man – too long, both in face and body. I have even penetrated the mysteries of Señor Alvarez. He is, as we thought, South American, and hides in his Hampstead fastness because of a small matter involving the treasury of his former Republic. I have failed to discover much about the Scots captain, save that he speaks with a Scottish accent, but I am more interested in Fuller and the yachtsman. Morrison's information points in their direction.'

We had turned back across the hilltop and now looked down through the trees to Holmes' villa beneath us, with its rows of beehives at the back and a straight plume of smoke rising from its chimney into the still winter air. Beyond it the Channel glinted like a sheet of dull, grey steel.

'We have a message, Watson,' said Holmes, and pointed with his stick to a uniformed youth pedalling away from the villa on a scarlet bicycle. We quickened our pace downward, and Martha met us at the door with a yellow envelope. It was a telegram from Mycroft:

INTERRUPTING YOUR HOLIDAY AT THREE TOMORROW AFTERNOON STOP MATTER MOST GRAVE AND URGENT STOP M

Holmes passed it to me with a smile. 'Really, Watson,' he remarked, 'if I were you this is the last place I would choose for a holiday!'

The carriage from Fulworth Station next day bore Mycroft, well wrapped in travelling rugs, but he was not alone. Beside him sat a man whose face was familiar from the daily papers – Mr Herbert Asquith.

'Mr Holmes,' said the Prime Minister, when Martha had

140

served tea in the drawing-room, 'your brother has told me that for some time you have been investigating the activities of German Intelligence in this country.'

'That is not quite true, Prime Minister,' said Holmes. 'For some time I have been aware of the activities of one of their agents, a man who has committed hideous crimes in this country, even in peacetime, and whose value to the Kaiser in wartime would be inestimable. With that in mind, and acting under the direct order of His Late Majesty, I have devoted some effort to identifying and neutralising this man before war comes.'

'And are you succeeding?' asked the Prime Minister.

'I draw closer to him by degrees. I must not frighten him away, lest he return in wartime in some other deadly guise, but I have every confidence that I shall find him.'

Mycroft cleared his throat uneasily. 'Sherlock,' he said, 'could you be persuaded to put aside – for the moment only – the pursuit of this man and divert your attention elsewhere?'

Holmes' eyes flashed like flints. 'There would have to be reasons of the most compelling nature,' he said.

'Then let me tell you what they are,' said the Prime Minister. 'When the Kaiser launches his war, his first target will be France or Russia. We are bound by agreements that make it impossible to stand aside in either case, even if we wished it. In particular, we are about to ratify an agreement with the French that, if they are attacked, our Fleet will hold the Channel and the North Sea against Germany.'

He paused, and his level eyes gazed across the darkening ocean beyond the windows.

'It is now a race to be ready. The Germans press on, building dreadnoughts and zeppelins, driving the Kiel Canal. We must not be behind them by one jot when the day comes.'

'Why should we be?' asked Holmes.

'Because, Mr Holmes, things have begun to go wrong – little things, perhaps, but important things. A dockyard accident here, an office fire there, a leakage of information elsewhere – small things, I say, but the totality adds up to espionage and sabotage and weakens and delays our efforts.'

'But my brother's office . . .' began Holmes.

'. . . has been actively pursuing these incidents and knows their sponsor,' said the Prime Minister.

141

'And who may that be?' asked Holmes of his brother.

'A German gentleman who settled in this country two years ago, who keeps a country house on the east coast and is principally renowned in England for his sporting interests,' replied Mycroft.

'Herr Maximilian von Bork, of Oakley Green in Essex,' said Holmes quietly.

The effect was astonishing. The Prime Minister set down his cup with a clatter and Mycroft groped in the wrong pocket for his snuffbox.

'You know him?' asked Mycroft incredulously.

'I know of him,' corrected Holmes. 'I know that he was the commissioner of the bomb that so nearly took your own life, and I know that he lies at the heart of the Kaiser's web in England. I know that beneath the bluff exterior that so charms the officers with whom he plays polo and the gentlemen with whom he rides to hounds, there operates the icy brain of a master-spy. I know that every German agent in this country reports to him, even if they do not know his name.'

'If you know so much of him, brother, it could be that what we are about to propose may be of more interest to you,' said Mycroft.

'Let me be quite clear, Mycroft,' said Holmes. 'I discovered von Bork in the course of my search for the railway maniac. I am interested in him only insofar as he will lead me to my quarry.'

'Then I see no difficulty,' said the Prime Minister. 'What I was about to put to you was this – it is not in our interests to stop von Bork at present.'

'With respect, sir, why ever not?' I asked.

'Because, doctor, if we stop him now we shall not know the names of those who report to him, and Berlin will replace von Bork with someone else we shall not know. We have a different plan – to turn their own agents against them as we identify them.'

'To infiltrate his organisation and feed him false information?' asked Holmes.

'Exactly, Mr Holmes,' said the Prime Minister.

There was a long pause, then Mycroft asked, 'Are you willing to do this thing, Sherlock?'

'On two conditions only,' said Holmes. Mycroft opened his mouth but Holmes stopped him with an imperious hand. 'No!' he said. 'My conditions are absolute and they are these – firstly, I must be allowed to proceed entirely as I wish, and secondly, no one but we four must know of this arrangement. Von Bork paid the man who infiltrated your office, Mycroft, and the risk is sufficient without that!'

Mycroft's relief at his brother's agreement battled on his features with hurt at the reference to Hugo, but the former won. Mr Asquith rose and shook Holmes warmly by the hand.

When our visitors had gone I turned to Holmes in dismay. 'Holmes,' I said, 'this is desperately dangerous! You are walking into the lions' den!'

'My dear Watson,' he said, 'I shall not make the mistake of appearing to him as a juicy morsel of meat – no, rather I shall confront him as another creature, fully as fierce and wily as himself, one that he had better make an ally. Besides, this is a marvellous opportunity to come at our maniac from another direction. After all, von Bork issues his orders.'

The following day Holmes surprised me by joining me on my return to London, and more so by suggesting that we take Emily Norton to supper that evening.

When we met he questioned Emily closely about the connections between the Kaiser's agents in America and the Irish Fenians there.

'Your great-uncle's banking enterprises must make him privy to all manner of information,' said Holmes. 'Would he be able to discover the identity of German agents who deal with the Irish in America?'

Emily gazed at him thoughtfully. 'If they move money through American banks,' she replied, 'Uncle Theo can find them out. Would you like me to ask him?'

'Only if it can be done with absolute confidentiality,' said Holmes. 'Tell your great-uncle that I am, in his own phrase, calling in his marker. I am sure he will supply any information he can obtain.'

I could see that Holmes' questions had disturbed Emily. As we left the restaurant she drew me aside.

'Doctor,' she said, 'what is Mr Holmes up to? If he tangles with the Fenians as well as the Kaiser's spies, I fear for him!'

'Dear lady,' I said, 'my lips are sealed on this matter. I can only say that it is his choice and that, in thirty years, I have never known him put his personal safety before his duty. He is the best and bravest man I have ever known.'

Holmes stayed at my home while he waited for news from Theobald G. Evans. It arrived within days, in the form of a telegram from the San Diego office of his bank. It mystified me entirely, for it read:

71	115	67	50	76	16	02	62	50	06	01	74	09	08
05	09	17	03	73	118	111	08	23	50	106	19	50	121
56	68	167	118	20	09	129	07	64	08	125	42	195	128
21	65	192	127	43	196	131	03	56	195	129	167	200	134
16	68	56	08	50	09	130	04	02	203	02	17	01	144
22	70	204	111	09	02	05	85	76	205	74	18	28	28
108	72	200	17	27	17	157	167	106	201	51	28	201	02
01	133	56	58	118	19	70	02	134	09	68	129	37	56
43	78	05	41	74	32	43	25	135	31	15	21	14	03
64	07	34	19	28	16	41							

'It is evidently a cipher,' I said, when Holmes showed it to me, 'but how do you propose to read it without a clue?'

'I have told you before, Watson, that all ciphers are constructed upon a few simple principles.'

'Yes,' I agreed. 'I recall that if the code is a simple substitution, as in replacing A by 1, B by 2 and so on, then the thing reveals itself by the known frequency of certain letters in English. Is that the case here? The figure 09 seems to appear fairly often. Does that represent E?'

'Good work, Watson!' he exclaimed. 'I see that my remarks are not entirely lost upon you, but this is not a simple substitution. In such codes the most frequently recurring symbol usually represents E as you suggest, and this can be confirmed by its appearance at the end of three-symbol sequences which stand for "the" and so on. Here there is no such structure. In addition, only twenty-six symbols are needed to substitute for the whole alphabet and there are far more than that here.'

'Then what kind of cipher is this?'

'A more complex one entirely,' said Holmes, 'but not one that is impossible to decipher, I think. For a start there is a useful error in the form of the message – two columns, one longer than the other.'

'I don't see the significance.'

'It is a usual practice to make the total of symbols in a message divisible by several numbers. It is then possible to write your message in a variety of square or rectangular shapes, without revealing where it begins or which way it runs. Thus a message of one hundred characters might be written as a square of ten by ten, or a rectangle of twenty by five, or two columns of five by ten. The text might begin at any corner and run in any direction. This message contains one hundred and thirty-three symbols, making it divisible only by seven and nineteen, not the most useful of numbers. Pray take a paper, Watson, and write the numbers in horizontal lines, taking the top number in the first left-hand column, then the top of the first right-hand column and so on.'

'How will this help us?' I asked, as I began the task.

'The asymmetrical layout suggests that the two columns were begun at the top left, most likely deriving from an original that was nineteen characters by seven. In the new form it will be easier to read.

'Now,' he continued, bending over my shoulder, 'the figures up to two hundred, with few repeats, suggest that this is based on a short piece of text. In that respect it is similar to the code we came across in the Birlstone affair, and cannot be read without the text from which it is derived. It could not be Mr Evans' intention that we should not read it, and so it must be a text he knows to be available to us. The usual sources are the Bible or Shakespeare . . .'

'Both of which are on the shelf, there,' I interrupted.

'. . . but it is neither of those,' Holmes continued.

'How can you tell?' I asked.

'There are a few symbols missing from the lower numbers. Thus 01 to 10 appear, in some cases more than once, but 11 to 14 are entirely absent. Is that not suggestive?'

'I cannot see it,' I admitted.

'My dear Watson! You are less than your best today! Four symbols in sequence – does that not suggest a date such as 1066 or 1492? There is no such date in the Bible or Shakespeare and we must look elsewhere.'

He straightened and gazed at my bookcases for a moment. 'Of

course!' he exclaimed. 'Evans told us that he read the American publications of your records. It must be a text that you have mentioned in those!' Seizing a volume from the cases, he began rapidly to flick through the pages.

'Could it not be one of your own works?' I asked. 'The Lassus book, *The Tracing of Footsteps*, or your paper on tobacco ashes?'

'I should not think so,' he replied. 'He sent his wire here. It must be something that he expects you to keep, Watson, not me.'

He pulled another volume from the shelf and leafed through it. 'Great heavens, Watson! You seem to have delighted in portraying me as almost illiterate!' he exclaimed impatiently. He was in the act of thrusting the book back into the case when he paused.

'I have it!' he cried. 'Watson! Take another paper and jot down these numbers!'

Pulling out yet another book and opening it, he began to call out letters and numbers. I was too busy recording them to make much sense of the text, but it seemed familiar.

When I had listed some two hundred letters and numbers he joined me at the table, and together we commenced to write in the letters against the columns of Evans' numbers.

We soon had this:

P	L	E	A	S	E	D	T	O	H	E	L	P	W	I	N
71	62	05	08	56	07	21	03	16	04	22	85	108	167	01	02
N	E	N	B	U	R	G	A	N	D	S	A	N	D	E	R
43	25	64	115	50	09	23	68	64	65	56	68	02	70	76	72
S	A	R	E	M	E	N	Y	O	U	W	A	N	T	S	A
106	133	134	78	135	07	67	06	17	50	167	08	192	195	56	203
N	D	E	R	S	R	E	C	R	U	I	T	S	F	E	N
204	205	200	201	56	09	05	31	34	50	01	03	106	118	125	127
I	A	N	S	C	O	N	T	A	C	T	M	E	C	O	M
129	08	02	111	74	17	51	58	68	41	15	19	76	74	73	19
Y	N	E	W	Y	O	R	K	O	F	F	I	C	E	F	O
20	42	43	167	50	17	09	18	27	28	118	129	74	21	28	16
R	F	U	R	T	H	E	R	I	N	F	O	R	M	A	T
09	118	50	09	195	196	200	09	01	02	28	17	201	19	37	32
I	O	N	A	S	S	I	S	T	A	N	C	E	F	U	N
14	16	02	08	111	121	129	128	131	134	130	144	05	28	157	02
D	S	E	T	C											
70	56	43	03	41											

'What have we here?' he mused, when the transliteration was complete. 'A little punctuation, Watson, and we have a clear message.' On a third piece of paper he wrote:

> Pleased to help – Winnenburg and Sanders are men you want – Sanders recruits Fenians – contact me c/o my New York office for further information, assistance, funds, etc.

'It is absurdly simple!' I exclaimed.

'As Christopher Columbus remarked of an egg, Watson, it is always absurdly simple when you have been shown how. No matter – like Columbus I shall now cross the Atlantic, now that I have the assurance of Theobald Evans' assistance.'

'The Atlantic!' I said. 'But von Bork is here in Essex!'

'The web of German intrigue is spun across the world, Watson, from Berlin to Lisbon and Amsterdam, to Brussels and St Petersburg, to New York and Chicago. I shall approach von Bork from its outer edges and by the time I reach his corner he will accept me as one its natural denizens. Now I must wire a reply and arrange to sail as soon as may be.'

He dashed off about his business, leaving me to ponder on the dangers which might face him in America, and to wish with all my heart that I was sailing with him.

He had been gone about an hour when a second message arrived from Theobald G. Evans, this time from his Tucson office. It turned out to be the key to the cipher and read:

MR SHERLOCK HOLMES STOP A RED CONTEMPLATION IN THE HOUSE-HOLD MANAGERESS YEARBOOK STOP EVANS

I admit, to my embarrassment, that it took me some long time to realise to which text it referred.

22

THE FLEET GOES NORTH

Within days of receiving the banker's message Holmes had sailed from Southampton. I did not even have the chance of a dockside farewell, for he travelled in disguise and under an assumed name.

Apart from the years after the Reichenbach affair, Holmes' pursuit of von Bork brought about the longest separation in our long partnership, and in some ways it was harder to bear. When I had thought him dead, I mourned him deeply, but I knew, or I thought that I knew, that he had gone to his death willingly and fearlessly, to remove a scourge from the earth. Now I was filled with foreboding for him. I could not know where he was or what he was about, save that he was moving among men who would kill if they so much as suspected treachery. I feared that he might come to some squalid and unacknowledged end somewhere and that I should never know the manner of his passing.

I took to scanning the news from America minutely, hoping that I might glean some small item that would reveal my friend's hand, but without success. Finding myself one evening in the vicinity of the Diogenes Club, I was emboldened to call on Mycroft Holmes. He welcomed me affably enough, but if he knew his brother's whereabouts he did not tell me.

In this uneasy, empty fashion two years went slowly by. In the spring of 1914 the war talk grew louder when Germany completed the Kiel Canal. Now the fleet of dreadnoughts she had been amassing for years had direct access to the North Sea, and only the most obstinately optimistic could believe that war was far away. In the summer a detachment of our Fleet visited Germany, where the Kaiser had the effrontery to review them in the uniform of a British admiral, and to express again his respect and affection for England.

The weather made that summer one to linger in the memory, and in the dust and smell of the capital I thought often of Holmes' airy drawing-room with its wide view of the ocean. I acquired a motor car and learned to drive it myself on trips into the countryside, but I would not stay long away from home lest I miss some news of my friend.

Then, in late June, came the spark that was to ignite the powder train. At Serajevo in the Balkans, the Archduke Franz Ferdinand, Heir Apparent to the Austrian Empire, was shot down with his Duchess by a member of the Black Hand, a Serbian nationalist society. As I stood in a sunlit London street, reading the news, my mind ran back to the dining-room at Balmoral on an autumn night, where King Edward had expressed his fear that a bullet fired at the wrong prince or politician would undo all his careful negotiations.

I sat, one sweltering July afternoon, rereading the news, which grew darker each day. Germany had offered her support to Austria. Reparations had been demanded from Serbia and their reply rejected by Austria. Now no one could doubt that the Balkans would explode and all Europe would take fire from them.

I heard a bicycle laid against my front railings and the door bell jangled. Louisa soon carried in a telegram. Its contents brought me to my feet, grinning like a fool. It read:

COME TO THE VILLA AT SEVEN TONIGHT STOP TRAVEL BY MOTOR CAR STOP COME ALONE APART FROM ADAMS THE BULLDOG STOP UTMOST SECRECY STOP HOLMES

I sent Louisa to pack my bag with such urgency that she believed some calamity had occurred and could not reconcile it with my fatuous grin, while I rushed to the garage to start up my Ford. When the bag was ready I paused only to include my trusty Adams .450 before setting off for Sussex.

Once London was behind me, the wind on my face was a delight as I headed south, like a schoolboy given a sudden holiday. Soon I was in the network of narrow lanes that lead to the Sussex coast and, a little before seven, I turned at the wooden fingerpost that marks the route to Fulworth. I passed through the little village street, pursued by cheering children, and pulled up the rise towards Holmes' villa, arriving at his gate precisely on time.

Springing from the motor, I pushed up my dusty goggles and dashed into the porch. I had my hand on the bell-pull when the front door swung suddenly open to reveal a tall, sun-bronzed stranger with a small goatee beard.

'Well, hello there,' he said, in a sharp Yankee drawl. 'You must be the Dr Watson I've heard so much about. You're very welcome!'

Nonplussed, I mumbled words of greeting and shook the proffered hand, while wondering who this might be.

'I'm Sherlock's American cousin, Otis T. Pennybanker,' said the American. 'But you must be weary after your drive. Come in and let me get you some vittles.'

I knew of no transatlantic cousin of Holmes, but I reflected that it had been years before he had introduced me to Mycroft, so I followed my host into the villa's hall, where he turned and smiled broadly at me. As he did so the face of Otis Pennybanker underwent a remarkable transformation, reforming itself into the features of my friend.

'Watson!' he cried. 'How extremely good to see you!'

I shook my head in wonderment at the complete deception, and, grasping his hand again in both of mine, wrung it warmly.

'Holmes!' I said. 'You cannot imagine how relieved I am to see you, dear fellow!'

'At least the offer of refreshment was authentic,' said Holmes, and led me into the villa's big, red-tiled kitchen. 'I am afraid that Martha is away for a while, but her niece serves me and I am sure there is something for us.'

We sat in two wooden armchairs at a corner of Martha's big, scrubbed wooden table, while Holmes served us from a jug of local brew and uncovered a plate of beef sandwiches. When the cool ale had washed the dust from my throat I asked the first of many questions.

'What on earth is the beard for?'

Holmes chuckled drily. 'In Fulworth it enables me to pass as my cousin, who has spent this summer here, thereby concealing my presence. In my dealings with Herr von Bork it has helped me to pass as Dennis O'Neill Altamont, an Irish-American with a pronounced distaste for England.'

'Then you have been in England some time?' I asked.

'For a year or so,' said Holmes, 'but I did not dare make contact with you, lest I brought danger on us both. Now the game is drawing to its end and I cannot do without my old colleague. Within days von Bork will be mine and then I shall learn the secret of the astronomer.'

The sun sank while we sat in Martha's kitchen and Holmes retailed to me his exploits. Theobald G. Evans had offered an introduction to Sanders, who organised disaffected Irishmen as agents for the Kaiser. Evans had warned Holmes that Sanders was scrupulous in his enquiries into the background of his agents, so Holmes had taken pains to pass any test. Travelling to Chicago he had taken work in a meat-packing manufactory, where he made no secret of his anti-English sentiments among his Irish fellow workers. At length he was invited to join the Fenian Brotherhood, and in a grotesque ceremony of knives and skulls had entered that secret order and soon become one of its most trusted brothers.

We moved to Holmes' study and lit the lamps and our pipes while he told me how, armed with his Chicago reputation, he had moved to Buffalo and contacted the Fenians again. It was not long before Sanders singled him out for a small mission in Ireland. His mission completed, he had taken a leaf out of Birdy Edwards' book and been publicly arrested after a battle with two constables in Skibbereen. Dragged away to gaol shouting abuse of King George, he was released when his bail (and subsequently his fines) were paid by an agent of von Bork.

So it was that he had arrived at von Bork's lair thoroughly accredited. Never doubting him for a moment, von Bork had instructed him to set up as a motor mechanic and, in time, had made Holmes one of his most highly paid agents. With Mycroft's assistance Holmes had fed the Prussian false information, while gradually learning the identities of many of his fellow agents.

'This all sounds hideously dangerous, Holmes!' I exclaimed.

'Tut, Watson!' he replied. 'You yourself have never flinched from danger, my friend, and it has always been a dimension of my profession. If I confined myself to rationalisation and deduction from an armchair I should be as bad as brother Mycroft!'

'Where is von Bork now?' I enquired.

'Still in Essex, blissfully unaware that he is watched, and waiting for two things – my delivery of the new Naval Codes and word from Carlton House Terrace that his mission is ended and he can go home.'

'Do you have the new Naval Codes?' I asked.

Holmes nodded towards a wrapped parcel in a pigeon-hole of his desk and smiled. 'There is something there that will pass for the codebook as long as is necessary. When Mycroft sends word that the time is ripe – and I have had to suffer the intrusion of the telephone so that he can do so – you and I will put an end to von Bork's game.'

By the third day of my visit there was still no news from Mycroft. We had risen late and sat late at breakfast, reading the newspapers. The Balkan news grew worse, Austria having declared war on Serbia. Now Russia would assist Serbia and Germany would combine with Austria.

Behind Holmes the open window let in the scent of a warm summer morning. I was turning a page of my paper when something on the horizon caught my eye.

'What is that, Holmes?' I asked, and pointed.

He turned in his chair, lowering his newspaper, then rose and stepped to the window. After watching for a while in silence, he turned to me.

'I believe that is the first sign of war,' he said. 'Let us go outside.'

We walked on to the cliff top, where a number of villagers were already gathered. Others were running up the lane from the village. All of their eyes were on the western horizon, where long shapes lay in a line across the sea. As we came amongst them they turned worried faces to us.

'What is it, doctor?' asked one. 'What's 'appening?'

As I looked out across the water there was no doubting what those shapes were – they were vessels of His Majesty's Fleet, steaming up the Channel in battle order.

'Is it war?' another Sussex voice asked.

Doctors are practised in telling kindly untruths, but I suspect my voice carried little conviction as I said, 'No, no. Not war. The Fleet has been on manoeuvres and come back to Portland. Now parts of it are going elsewhere.'

Holmes looked at me with one eyebrow raised. He had brought field-glasses with him, and now scanned each vessel closely. After a while he put the glasses into my hand and turned back to the house.

How long I stood on the cliff top I do not know, but the line of warships grew until it extended all the way across our horizon. A steady breeze blew from the south-west, but the standards at bows and mastheads streamed stiffly back against it, as the vessels made all speed to the east. To us their passing was silent, but one could imagine the throb of the mighty engines that drove them across the sunlit sea.

There were destroyers, small and lean, around the outside of the line, with here and there the turret of a submarine, its small deck awash from its own speed and a handful of its crew clinging to the superstructure, while at the heart of the procession sailed the great battleships, including *Dreadnought* herself, moving like a Queen among her sisters named for her. With the glasses I could see that I had spoken less than the truth to the villagers, for every gun position was cleared for action.

There must have been fifteen or twenty miles of ships, all pressing east with dark smoke streaming aft from their funnels, and I knew this was no detachment homeward bound after manoeuvres – this was the seaborne might of England going to its battle stations, ready for war. More than any commentary in any newspaper it made me realise that there would be no turning back.

As the line tailed away to the east, I turned back to the villa, thinking that there had been no European war since my child-hood. I recalled Mycroft's prophecies and a chill went through me at the thought of those miles of war machinery pounding their way towards the North Sea.

Holmes met me at the door. 'Mycroft has telephoned,' he said. 'The Austrians have attacked Belgrade and the Russians have mobilised on the Austrian frontier. Churchill has sent the Fleet to Scapa Flow, so they will not be trapped in the Channel when it begins. Mycroft expects to give us the word at any moment.'

So we waited while the storm gathered momentum. The

French Army moved to within ten kilometres of their frontier, determined not to provoke the Germans. Our Prime Minister called on France and Germany to guarantee the neutrality of Belgium, but the Kaiser did not respond.

The August Bank Holiday weekend began, while diplomatic move and countermove continued. On Saturday afternoon France and Germany moved to general mobilisation and, early that evening, two companies of German troops entered Luxembourg in motorcars, while Germany declared war on Russia. Late that night Mycroft telephoned.

When Holmes replaced the earpiece his face was grim. 'Tomorrow night,' he said, 'we shall keep our appointment with von Bork.'

23

THE SPIDER TRAPPED

I must now apologise to all of my readers. I do not know if the name of Sherlock Holmes will be remembered when this manuscript is published – though it would be a grave injustice if he were forgotten. If he is still remembered, and if my previous records of his cases are still extant, then some of you will have read 'His Last Bow: the War Service of Sherlock Holmes', in which there appears an account of the taking of von Bork. To you I apologise for the omissions and alterations in that narrative. It was written at the insistence of Mycroft Holmes and its purpose, as he conceived it, was to encourage my friend's many followers in their own war efforts by revealing something of Holmes' part in the struggle. At the same time he demanded that I conceal the whole story of the astronomer. As a result I was forced to take a number of liberties with the truth and, in the end, I was so dissatisfied with the result that I rewrote the story in the third person, since it was by no means my recollection of events.

To those readers to whom the story of von Bork is completely new, I must also apologise, for much that is in 'His Last Bow' is true, and I do not propose to repeat all of it here.

Suffice it to say that Holmes and I left Fulworth in my motor on the morning of Sunday, 2nd August, and arrived in the vicinity of von Bork's estate at about nine in the evening. It had been another hot day, and the twilight was sultry and oppressive. On the hill above Oakley Green we halted, while Holmes took the field-glasses and scanned the area beyond the village.

'There are lights on the ground floor,' he said, 'and a lighted window above, which is my faithful spy's signal.'

'You have a spy in von Bork's own household?' I exclaimed.

Holmes chuckled. 'You have not asked why I am doing without the services of the estimable Martha,' he said. 'She is Herr von Bork's housekeeper!'

'Martha!' I ejaculated. 'Holmes, how could you place her within that man's reach?'

'She is quite safe, Watson,' he replied. 'There is a good deal more cunning in her head than is needed in her kitchen. She observes our spider for me and keeps track of his letters. Tonight she will let me know when he is alone.'

Suddenly a light blinked out in the darkness beyond the village. 'There!' cried Holmes. 'Martha's signal! Let us go!'

I started the car and we ran swiftly through the little village and into a lane at its far end. Rounding a bend in the lane we were suddenly blinded by the lights of a great vehicle coming at us in the centre of the road. It took all of my skill to keep us out of the ditch, as an enormous 100 horsepower Benz rushed by us.

As I cursed the driver of the Benz, Holmes laughed. 'That was Baron von Herling, the Chief Secretary of the Legation. Our prey is now alone.'

I pulled up at the gate in front of the dark bulk of the house and Holmes sprang out, taking with him a parcel he had brought from Sussex. 'Wait for my call, Watson,' he commanded, 'and keep your pistol handy!'

I lit a cigarette and settled to my wait. It was only some fifteen minutes later that Holmes called me from the gate: 'Bring the luggage straps, Watson!' I followed him into the house and into a book-lined study.

A powerful, aquiline-featured man lay on the floor and the room reeked of chloroform. Above the table a wall-safe stood open. 'Faugh!' I exclaimed, wrinkling my nose at the familiar smell. 'What have you been doing, Holmes?'

'I am afraid', he said, 'that Herr von Bork was so upset when he discovered that it was not the Naval Codes for which he had just paid five hundred pounds that he was quite overcome,' and he pointed to the table.

I saw the wrapper of Holmes' parcel on the table, together with a small blue book. The title, embossed in gold, was *A Practical Handbook of Bee Culture, with some Observations on the Segregation of the Queen*.

I chuckled. 'So you sold him your book instead!'

'Indeed, Watson, and I am left with a pretty profit over the printer's bill. Now, be so kind as to assist me with the luggage straps before our prisoner recovers.'

We soon had the Prussian trussed and laid on the sofa. Holmes helped me to a celebratory glass of the prisoner's best wine and began to cram documents from the safe into a valise. Martha joined us and it was a pleasure on that bizarre night to see her unruffled features and to know that she was safe. Before she left, Holmes thanked her warmly for her efforts and asked her to await us at Claridge's Hotel the next morning.

Von Bork now recovered consciousness and proceeded to curse Holmes in a voluble stream of German; nor was he greatly mollified to learn that he had been betrayed not by Dennis O'Neill Altamont, but by Sherlock Holmes. His struggles made it difficult to move him, but eventually we packed him and the valise of documents into the motor and set out for London, where we delivered our prisoner to Scotland Yard before making for our hotel.

The next day, Bank Holiday Monday, dawned grey and damp, though still warm. Bad news continued – the Germans had occupied Luxembourg and given Belgium twelve hours to decide if she would allow the German Army to pass through and attack France. Martha attended us while we were still at breakfast, bringing lists of addresses on letters that von Bork had sent or received. Holmes scanned them anxiously, comparing them with his list of suspects, but finding no similarities. As Martha set out for Sussex we took a cab to Scotland Yard.

On our way it became evident that the holiday had not reduced the crowds in London. So far from emptying the capital, the last few days' events seemed to have drawn people into the city, wanting, perhaps, to be close to the seat of affairs at this perilous time.

At the Yard a plain-clothes inspector of the Political Branch met us and showed us into a room not far from the entrance. Through two tall windows came the faint sound of traffic on the Embankment. There was a plain desk, some bookcases, a few chairs upholstered in red and, in front of the desk, a large brown leather armchair.

'Where is the prisoner?' asked Holmes.

'We've got him in the cells at Cannon Row, sir. We can have him here in a moment,' said the Inspector, 'and the Chief said I was to be outside with two armed constables while he's here, sir.'

'Very wise,' said Holmes. 'Watson, pray take that armchair. Inspector, you may bring in the prisoner.'

A few minutes later two uniformed officers, each with a pistol at his belt, marched the handcuffed von Bork into the room. He was pale under his tan, but more composed than on the previous night. As he stood between his guards he wished us a curt 'Good-day!'

'I trust that it will be,' said my friend. 'Officer, please let him sit in the brown armchair and release his handcuffs.'

'Are you sure, sir?' asked one of the constables.

'My colleague here has a loaded pistol and you two will be immediately outside. I do not think our guest will be so foolish as to attempt escape.'

The officers seated their prisoner and unlocked his handcuffs. As they withdrew Holmes told them, 'I expect some papers to be delivered. Please see that I have them as soon as they arrive.'

Von Bork rubbed his chafed wrists and watched Holmes. 'I was less than polite to you last night, Mr Holmes,' he said. 'I apologise. You were right to say that each of us had done what we could for our country.'

'Now, that is more sporting of you,' said Holmes, 'and I hope it presages a useful conversation.'

'Please do not misunderstand me,' said the Prussian. 'I am your prisoner. You may do with me what you will, but nothing you can do will persuade me to assist the enemies of the Fatherland.'

'There is little information in your head which we did not invent or which we do not know,' said Holmes, 'but there is one matter in which you can assist us . . .'

The German began to protest, but Holmes cut him short.

'Hear me out!' he commanded. 'The man whose office this is holds the power of life and death over you. If he permits, you might yet return to Germany when the last boat leaves with your colleagues. If not, you may at best spend the war in a cell, or at worst end in the execution shed at Pentonville or leave a few more bullet-holes in a certain wall in the Tower of London.'

'You would not hang me!' expostulated von Bork. 'That would be outrageous!'

'It would certainly be unfortunate from your point of view, but I have nothing to do with it. You are, as I say, worthless to British Intelligence. It would be easy to make an example of you. On the other hand, my enquiries relate to one matter only and, if you help me, I will certainly recommend to our authorities that you be treated leniently.'

'And what is this one matter?' asked von Bork warily.

'You have employed an Englishman, an explosives expert, on a number of occasions. My interest is in him.'

'What makes you think there is such a man?' asked von Bork.

'Do not waste my time!' snapped Holmes. 'And do not throw away your opportunities! If you want a firing-squad in the Tower moat it can be arranged very quickly! There is such a man and I was aware of him before I knew of you. He was active before you set foot in this country. The Portland explosion was his handiwork, as was the fire at Barrow-in-Furness, and both of those were carried out on your orders!'

'If you know so much, you must know that different agents carried out the Portland and Barrow operations,' said von Bork.

'With devices of great cunning, both evidently manufactured by the same hand – as was the device used at the Diogenes Club,' said Holmes.

There was a tap at the door and one of the uniformed constables entered with a large manilla envelope which he gave to Holmes.

'I am not going to help you protect your dockyards and factories,' said von Bork, 'nor even your gentlemen's clubs! In days – perhaps in hours – our countries will be at war. You have said you understand what I have done. Then you must understand why I cannot assist you!'

'I am dealing with things done years ago,' said Holmes grimly. 'I am not dealing with the sabotage of shipyards, naval docks and manufactories, but with slaughterous attacks on innocent women and children!'

Before von Bork could reply, Holmes snatched up the envelope and tore it open, allowing its contents to slither across the

159

desk in front of the Prussian. I leaned forward and then recoiled as I saw the images scattered before us. The envelope had been full of photographs of the victims of the three railway disasters, more dreadful in the stark monochrome of photographs, perhaps, than in bloody reality.

'What are these, von Bork?' hissed Holmes. 'Are these the people against whom the All Highest makes war? Women, children, innocent travellers on the railway, destroyed or maimed by the work of your agent!'

The Prussian stared wide-eyed at the photographs before him. His hands moved as though of their own volition, picking up one after another and laying each down as its terrible image burned into his mind.

'This is not the work of my men!' he said at last. 'We have not done these things!'

'These things were done by your country's Intelligence Service before you arrived here, von Bork,' said Holmes, and his voice was quiet but harsh. 'They were done by an English madman who makes his perverted talents available to you. If you will not assist me in finding him, then I shall assume that you approve of his handiwork, in which case I shall leave you to our authorities. I have nothing further to say.'

We sat in silence, while the German continued to shuffle the pictures and stare at them. A tugboat hooted on the Thames and a tramcar rattled by below the windows. At last von Bork pushed the dreadful pictures aside. When he spoke, his voice was dry in his throat. 'I have not used this man for such work,' he said. 'Believe me, Mr Holmes.'

'Who is he?' demanded Holmes.

'I do not know his name,' said von Bork.

'But you issued his orders. You must know how to contact him.'

'He would telephone every week,' said von Bork. 'He called himself just "The Astronomer". He had a code arranged with my predecessor.'

'You have spoken on the telephone?' said Holmes. 'Then you know his voice – how does he speak?'

'Like an Englishman, like an educated Englishman – there was nothing unusual.'

'What was the code?' demanded Holmes.

'There were seven tobacconists in London – one for each day of the week. He would call and whichever of us had a message would say, "There is a message for you," and name the street, so "a message at Westbourne Terrace" meant he should collect it on Wednesday and so on.'

'Give me the streets and the names of the shops!' said Holmes.

Von Bork recited them and Holmes scribbled them in his pocket-book. 'How did you obtain his devices?' he asked.

'The same way. I would leave instructions at one of the tobacconists and when the device was ready he would call and say there was a parcel at such-and-such street.'

'How did you pay him?' asked Holmes.

'Pay him?' repeated von Bork. 'He is not paid, Mr Holmes. I have never made payments to him.'

'Von Bork,' said my friend, rising from his chair, 'if you have told me the truth I will speak to our authorities and demand consideration for you. If not – you know the penalty.'

'Do not worry,' said the Prussian wearily. 'I have told you what I know of this madman. Why else would I tell you my country's secrets?'

'What has passed between us in this room is our affair, von Bork. Your information is for my use only. What you choose to tell our authorities, or indeed your own, is up to you. Congratulate yourself that you have purged your country's shame that she used such a man for such purposes,' said Holmes, and he slid the gruesome pictures back into their envelope. 'Now,' he said, striking the package with his hand, 'I must go and do the same for the country which spawned him.'

THE ELEVENTH HOUR

As we stepped out of Scotland Yard into the August sunlight, we became aware of the hum of people. Since our arrival the crowds had thickened. Now they overflowed the pavements and traffic was almost at a standstill. People stood or milled about, anxiously scanning newspapers or repeating any scrap of news or rumour.

Our progress was slow and eventually Holmes pulled out his watch and looked at it anxiously. 'I think I shall return to our hotel, Watson. I need to consider what von Bork has told us and there is, I think, very little time left to trap the astronomer. Be so kind as to call on Mycroft and let him know what has taken place this morning.'

We separated at the entrance to Mycroft's department, and I was soon in his long room, detailing the morning's events.

'And can Sherlock now identify his man?' he asked when I had done.

'I wish I could tell you,' I replied, quite honestly. 'He has eliminated many of the people on his list. I really don't know if he can now complete his analysis.'

'We are very close to the edge, doctor,' said Mycroft. 'This morning the Belgians began blowing up the Meuse bridges and railway tunnels on the Luxembourg frontier. If the Germans enter Belgium we must stand by our guarantees. It is inconceivable that Parliament will not take us to war. The Territorials and Reservists are being called up. Sherlock must stop this man. If he is not stopped before we mobilise he will be a devastating weapon against us. You have seen his handiwork among civilians, doctor – imagine what havoc he could wreak on troop trains and munitions shipments!'

We continued to discuss the state of affairs. Mycroft told me that the Conservatives had sent the Prime Minister a declaration that it would be fatal to the honour and security of Britain if we stood aside from war. The Liberal Cabinet had been in continuous session for hours and two members had resigned over the prospect of war as an ally of the Czar of Russia.

I was about to leave when Mycroft suggested I join him at the House of Commons, where the Foreign Secretary would speak at three. To avoid the throng in Whitehall we walked down to the House through Horseguards, but the crowd had spilled out of Downing Street and on to St James's Park. Our appearance caused a ripple through the mob, as had each coming or going throughout the morning.

I have never been in the House of Commons, before or since, but Mycroft assured me that the chamber was fuller than he had ever seen it. The Members' benches were filled and seats had been placed in the gangways for the overflow. The Diplomatic Gallery carried a full complement of ambassadors and we shared the Strangers' Gallery with a large part of the House of Lords. Around me I spied a good many faces familiar to me from newspapers and I could not help reflecting that I was at the hub of the world that afternoon, for all Europe was waiting for England's decision.

We peered at the faces on the Government bench, trying to read some sign in the attitude of the Prime Minister and his men, but without success. Asquith's face was as steady and unrevealing as it had been in Holmes' sitting-room. Lloyd George looked pale and older than his years, while the man of the hour, Lord Grey, looked haggard and exhausted.

When at last Grey rose the mutterings round us ceased and everyone strained to catch every word. He began slowly, emotionally, reminding the House of British interests, British honour, and British obligations. He outlined the discussions between us and France, emphasising that we had no formal obligation to France. He pointed out that France was bound by treaty to Russia, but that we were not party to that treaty. Around us the muttering arose again. Grey seemed to be pressing the case for England to stand aside. 'This is appalling,' somebody whispered. 'They're going to stay out!'

The Foreign Secretary went on to speak of our naval agreement with France, explaining that the French Fleet lay in the Mediterranean leaving the north-west coasts of France undefended.

'If the German Fleet comes down the Channel,' he said, 'bombarding and battering the undefended coasts of France, we cannot stand aside and see this going on – practically within sight of our eyes – with our arms folded, looking on, doing nothing!'

The Opposition cheered but the Liberals sat silent. He turned to the neutrality of Belgium, asking if we could stand by and witness 'the direst crime that ever stained the pages of history', without becoming participants in the crime.

Finally he returned to British interests. 'Consider what may be at stake. If France is beaten to her knees – if Belgium falls, and then Holland and then Denmark – if, in a crisis like this, we run away from these obligations of honour and interest as regards the Belgian treaty, I do not believe for a moment that at the end of the war we shall be able to undo what has happened in the course of the war, to prevent the whole of the west of Europe opposite to us falling under the domination of a single power. We should sacrifice our good name and reputation before the world and should not escape the most serious and grave economic consequences.'

So he placed the question in their hands, and they answered with a storm of cheers and applause. Lord Grey, they say, was no great orator, but I can only say that on that afternoon he held the greatest debating chamber in the world in his hand for more than an hour, and I know that mine were not the only moist eyes as that wave of applause crashed through the House.

'What will happen now?' I asked Mycroft, as we pushed our way through the crowd in Old Palace Yard.

'He has what he wanted,' said Mycroft. 'The House has accepted Belgium as the issue. Now he will give the Kaiser twenty-four hours to stop the invasion.'

'And will he?' I asked, with very little doubt of the answer.

'No,' he replied. 'Tomorrow night we shall go to war. Please tell my brother he has one day left.'

At Claridge's I found the table of our sitting-room littered with sheets of the list of suspects, scattered over a map of

London and a railway map. The air was thick and grey with the smoke of coarse shag tobacco and Holmes sprawled back on a couch, his pipe in his mouth and both eyes closed. 'Watson!' he greeted me as he opened his eyes. 'How long have we got?'

I gave him Mycroft's message. 'It will be sufficient,' he said, sucking on his pipe. 'Von Bork's information has been most useful.'

'Then you have identified our man?' I asked eagerly.

'Not quite,' he replied, 'but look at this,' and he rose and walked across to the table.

'Here are my suspects,' he said, picking up the sheets of his list. 'Now, Father Gallagher remains a possibility, though I confirmed that he has an Irish accent. Macleod I eliminated, and Alvarez, and von Bork eliminates Kelly, but his information points towards the teacher Scorfeld. Lennox I withdrew, and Miss Norton assured us it was not Miss Debenhoe. It might be the Reverend Corlett if he speaks South American Spanish, and Mr Bramwell is now a better proposition. Sheldon I investigated and he does not fit, but Sinclaire has become more interesting. Dr Barton has been eliminated and – thankfully – Captain Lymington-Keith.'

'Why thankfully?' I interjected.

'Because I should have had to spend a while passing myself off as a Highlander to find out about him. I fear the kilt and plaid would not become me!'

He ran his forefinger down the pages. 'Edwardes and Fuller are now far less likely. Miss Morgan we can leave to her unwed bliss and Mr Brown to his melodious poverty. We can now, I believe, make a more realistic list.'

Suiting the action to the words he jotted a few names in his pocket-book, then showed me the leaf:

Possibilities

Father Gallagher, Wilversall, Staffs
Scorfeld, Pawsley, Hants
Bramwell, Wokingham, Berks
Revd. Corlett, Stoke Mohun, Dorset
Sinclaire, Siddenton, Hants

'Is that not progress, Watson?' he asked as I scanned the list.

'It seems to be,' I said, 'but I cannot see what part von Bork's information has played. All I see is that four of them live in the south of England and one in the Black Country.'

'A thousand apologies!' said Holmes. 'I had forgotten that you were not here when I observed the pattern.'

'A pattern!' I exclaimed.

'In the seven tobacconists!' said Holmes, and he recited their locations, striking them off on his fingers. 'Monday was Maida Vale, Tuesday was Talbot Road, Wednesday was Westbourne Terrace, Thursday was Thurloe Street, Friday was Fitzroy Street, Saturday was Sussex Gardens and Sunday was St John's Wood Road. It is obvious, is it not?'

'Not to me, Holmes,' I said, shaking my head. 'They are all, I think, in the western part of London, but what of it?'

He seized me by the arm and pulled me back to the table. 'Look!' he cried, pointing at the street plan. 'There they are all marked, and there – in among them – is Paddington Station! The Great Western Railway terminus!'

His finger jabbed at the dark mass representing the huge station on the map and the seven red-pencilled crosses that marked the tobacconists' shops around it. 'Heavens, yes!' I exclaimed. 'I see it now. You believe he came to London by train, arriving always at Paddington, so that the contact addresses were within easy reach!'

'Precisely, Watson, and that is how I have reduced my list to five. I owe you another apology, old friend, for you once remarked that there might be something in where he lived. Unfortunately I have been forced to approach the problem from a different direction.'

'Is there any way of reducing the list further?' I asked.

'I am fairly certain that we can ignore Father Gallagher,' said Holmes. 'His parish lies between the Great Western connection at Birmingham and the Midland at Wolverhampton. I suspect he would travel by the latter and arrive at Euston.'

He picked up the railway map and surveyed it thoughtfully, tracing a line with one finger. 'We may also acquit the Vicar of Stoke Mohun. His living is close to the South-Western station at Yeovil. Now Scorfeld – where is Pawsley, Watson? It is not shown on this map.'

'It is to the north of the Meon valley, in East Hampshire,' I replied.

'Hmm,' said Holmes, and returned to his study of the map. 'Then we cannot eliminate our teacher. He might use the main line from Petersfield to Waterloo, but it would be no great exercise to cover his tracks by travelling from Basingstoke and changing lines at Reading, where the Great Western and Southern stations are immediately adjacent. No – we cannot ignore him.'

'What of the others?' I asked.

'Bramwell is at Wokingham, close to the main West of England line, and Sinclaire lives near a halt on the Didcot and Southampton, only a few miles from the Great Western at Newbury. They are both likely suspects.'

'What will you do now?' I enquired.

'I must think, Watson – I must go over the whole pattern. There must be some way of defining one of these last three!' and he flung his long form back on to the couch.

We did not dine that evening, but had a cold meal sent to our suite. Even so, Holmes barely touched it. He sat immobile, his face a mask and his eyes staring into space, while the air in the room thickened with pipe-smoke.

About the middle of the evening a hubbub in the streets below and the cries of news-vendors caused me to send out for a paper. Smeared headlines told of Germany's declaration of war on France, justified by lying stories of French aviators breaching Belgian neutrality. I passed the newspaper to Holmes without a word.

'It seems strange', I said, when he had absorbed the news, 'to think how we set out to discover the cause of a railway accident. Who could have guessed when we went to Temple Combe –'

I got no further, for Holmes uncoiled from the sofa like a spring. He stood with starting eyes and face as white as chalk. 'Temple Combe, Watson!' he cried. 'There is our confirmation – Temple Combe!'

'What on earth has Temple Combe to do with it now?' I cried.

'It has everything to do with it, Watson. Ah, my dear old friend, I have said before that you are not yourself luminous but you admit light, Watson, you admit light!'

167

He rang for a page and dashed off a telegram. When the message had gone he returned to his seat, and sat smiling and rubbing his hands.

'Holmes,' I pleaded, 'will you be good enough to tell me what is going on?'

'I should, I suppose, despair that after all the years you have observed my methods you have learned so little!' he replied. 'Elimination is the short answer! We have three suspects left, of which I regard the teacher Scorfeld as unlikely. Now we have a means of confirming which of the other two it may be – if either.'

'And if it is neither?'

'Then it must be the third – Scorfeld!' he snapped. 'Really, Watson, do you think you could refrain from questioning the obvious long enough to join me for a belated dinner?'

There was one more question, the answer to which did not seem obvious to me, and I asked it.

'What was the content of your telegram?'

'It was an enquiry to the Vicar of Temple Combe, asking to which magazines he subscribed in 1906,' declared Holmes. It made no manner of sense to me, but I forbore to question him further.

No reply had arrived by the time I made my way to bed, and for a long time after I retired I heard my friend pacing the sitting-room.

I awoke early, conscious that this must be the last day of our enquiry, and found Holmes drinking cup after cup of strong coffee at the breakfast table.

A page brought a telegram before we had finished breakfast. Holmes ripped it open impatiently and leapt up from the table with it in his hand. His eyes gleamed and he struck the open form with the back of his other hand. 'Come, Watson!' he commanded. 'To the reading room!'

I stumbled after him to the hotel's reading room, where he demanded from the assistant the first half-year volume for 1906 of a particular periodical.

Leafing rapidly through it with his long fingers he paused suddenly. Before the eyes of the shocked reading room attendant he ripped out two pages and crammed them into his pocket. Before the man could utter a syllable of protest, Holmes had flung him more coins than would pay for a new volume and whirled towards me.

'We have him, Watson!' he cried, raising the heads of a few early morning readers. 'We have our maniac! Come, Watson – the game's afoot!'

HIS OWN PETARD

The doorman was handing a lady from a cab as we ran out of the hotel's entrance, but Holmes could not wait. 'Paddington, cabby!' he shouted, as we tumbled pell-mell into another hansom. 'At your best speed!'

We jolted back in our seats as the driver whipped up his horse and turned into the crowded streets. The Bank Holiday was over, but numbers of people still loitered on the pavements. Union Jacks and patriotic signs had appeared on shop-fronts and hawkers peddled red, white and blue ribbon favours to the crowds. In one street we were delayed by a group of marching men, all in shirt-sleeves in the hot morning and carrying luggage. A small crowd bearing Union Jacks and tricolours and a band escorted them, and the banner at their head proclaimed them as French waiters going home to enlist.

At Paddington Holmes leapt from the cab and flung the cabby a handful of coins, then strode rapidly into the station. I raced after him along a platform and we flung ourselves into a compartment of a train that was just departing.

As the train pulled out of the dark vault of the station and we settled ourselves, Holmes drew from his pocket a small red book and began to thumb through it. At last he smiled to himself and returned it to his pocket.

'You have not, I hope, come unarmed?' he enquired.

I patted my pocket by way of confirmation. 'You think it will be needed?' I asked.

'It is as well to be prepared,' he said. 'We are, after all, dealing with a maniac.'

He spoke no further word, but closed his eyes and gave every appearance of being asleep. I watched the landscape and sought, unsuccessfully, to work out which of Holmes' propositions had been confirmed. We were pulling into Reading when Holmes opened his eyes, flung open the door and dropped down on to the platform before the train had come to rest. Jumping down after him, I followed him to a small side platform, where a local train was about to depart and then, at last, I knew our destination.

The little train brought us eventually to the racing town of Newbury, where we disembarked. A stable close to the station supplied a carriage, and soon we were trundling up the high hill, lined with handsome villas, that carries the Winchester road out of the town.

Leaving the town behind we splashed through the Enborne's waters at Sandleford, cheered by village children paddling beside the graceful wooden bridge. We were now on a long stretch of open road in Hampshire where we made good speed until, a few miles south of the border, our road twisted between the great green slopes of the downs. Just beyond, Holmes swung our equipage into a narrow, winding lane, white with the chalk dust of the ancient hills.

The banks around us were high and green with the summer growth of hedgerow and grass. Above us broad oaks spread their leaves, throwing the road into deep shadow. Between their trunks we could see fields of ripening corn spreading over the lower slopes of the hills. It affected me deeply to think that we rode through that beautiful countryside, drowsing in the hot quiet of a high summer afternoon, on our way to confront a homicidal madman.

The lane carried us past a tiny railway station, where we overtook a lady on a bicycle, pedalling furiously in the warm noonday. A few more twists of the lane brought us to the pillared gates of Siddenton Manor, and Holmes turned into the drive. Beyond the roadside trees a handsome Elizabethan manor house, of medium size, lay with its back to a spur of the hills. An elderly bulldog slept on the well-kept lawn and the gravelled drive was neat and weeded.

Holmes pulled at the big iron bell-pull beside the black oak front door, and somewhere within we heard an answering jangle. After a moment the door swung open to reveal, not the expected servant, but a gentleman of medium height, clad in a loose linen jacket. His face, under a thinning crop of brown hair, now greying, bore an expression of polite enquiry and his mild brown eyes were partly concealed by half-moon spectacles. Somewhat old-fashioned sidewhiskers and a small beard framed his features. He was just such a man as one might see in any court, rising from a nest of documents to address a judge with measured tones. Nothing in his manner or appearance suggested any kind of unbalance, but there was no doubting that we were face to face with the astronomer himself. He answered every particular of the descriptions we had been given.

'Please excuse me, gentlemen,' he said, 'but my staff are absent at present and I must do my own errands. Do please come in.'

He led us into the low hall of his home, where ancient leaded windows admitted the sunlight to sparkle on glass cases of exhibits. Holmes started towards one of the cases, hand out-stretched, drawing his little red book from his pocket.

'Forgive me, Mr Sinclaire,' he said. 'It is Mr Sinclaire, isn't it? It was precisely these specimens about which I came to enquire. The Railway Companion mentions that there are specimens from the chalk-pits to be seen in the County Museum, but that there are finer specimens in your own collection. My friend and I have come from the station here with a view to examining the Ancient British remains at Seven Barrows, but I felt we must risk intruding upon you if it gave us a chance to see your fossils!'

Sinclaire smiled at my friend's gushing enthusiasm. 'I shall be delighted to show them to you,' he said. 'It is only a short walk to the pits where these were obtained. Perhaps when you have examined them we might take a look at the scene of their exhumation?'

'That would be most kind, Mr Sinclaire,' said Holmes, and he and our host began a discussion of fossils that left me confused. When I had kept up a pretended interest for some thirty minutes Sinclaire suggested we examine the chalk-pits.

He led us out through the rear of the house and along the side of an old-fashioned kitchen garden. At the bottom a wicket gate opened on to a grassy path leading towards the railway.

'My father', he was explaining, 'was a railway engineer. He spent many years in South America, where I also spent my youth. When it came time for me to take up my education in this country, he retired here, but not entirely. The chalk-pits belong with the Manor and provided my father with an interest in his old age. Although I was trained to the law, I abandoned my practice some years since. Now I devote myself to my lifelong obsessions – the science of the stars and the science of the earth. In between these two harmonious pursuits I manage this little enterprise. Normally there would be three or four of my men here, but they have been so alarmed by the news that I have let them go into Litchfield to keep abreast of affairs.'

We had reached the railway embankment, and beyond it we could see where large embrasures had been blasted and cut into the hillside, revealing the raw, white chalk. An iron gate at the foot of the bank led to a flight of wooden steps that climbed the railway embankment to a wooden crossing of the country type. Sinclaire politely held the gate aside and followed us up the bank.

We were stepping on to the railway line when Sinclaire's amiable chatter ceased. When he spoke again it was with a new and different tone. 'Do not turn round, gentlemen!' he commanded. 'There is a loaded gun in my pocket!'

'Whatever do you mean, Mr Sinclaire?' began Holmes, but Sinclaire interrupted.

'You may drop your pretence, Mr Holmes,' he said. 'I know who you are and I know that you have been tracking me for some time and it is far too late in the game for any mistakes. I have long known that one day we should meet.'

'And now that we have,' said Holmes, 'what do you propose to do?'

'You and the good doctor are about to become the centre of one final mystery, Mr Holmes. Alas, Dr Watson will never add it to his records and it will remain forever unsolved. When the lime-pit yonder has done with you there will be no trace at all.'

'Don't be a fool!' said Holmes, turning to face Sinclaire. 'Do you think the county police are not already on their way here?'

Sinclaire laughed mockingly. 'You passed no police station on your way here. You are alone,' he said.

'We are here at the behest of my brother's department,' said

Holmes, 'whose resources are sometimes greater than a county police force.'

The madman laughed again. 'Your brother's operatives have hunted me for years without success. They will not save you – and once you are out of the way they will not prevent me from carrying out my work – work that can be really useful at last!'

'Do you call killing innocent people by stealth your "work"?' I exclaimed.

'Now, Watson!' said Holmes. 'You are, after all, a doctor. You should be able to make allowance for the fact that Mr Sinclaire is insane, though not, I hope, too insane for a rope in Pentonville.'

Sinclaire sprang towards Holmes and dragged his pistol from his pocket. 'What do you know of me? How dare you call me insane?' he snarled, his face whitening with rage.

'I fancy I know quite a bit about you,' said Holmes evenly. 'I know, for instance, that your involvement with Germany arises because your father married a German lady while working in that country, and that you were actually born in Dresden. I know that you and your mother followed your father's work all over the world until she died in a cholera epidemic in the Argentine in 1881 –'

'Do not speak of my mother!' screeched Sinclaire. His face streamed with sweat and the mild brown eyes now flashed strangely yellow. 'She did not "die", Holmes! She was murdered by a callous and selfish brute who thought more of steam pressures and coefficients of expansion than he did of his devoted wife! – a vain obsessive who dragged that gentle lady to places unfit for any woman, while she followed, uncomplaining, and her body and spirit wore out! Stop your damned babbling and move! *Cuando se acabo la cosa, se acabo la cosa*! It is finished, let it be finished! Now move!' and he brandished the pistol at Holmes.

While Holmes distracted Sinclaire I had managed to slip my hand on to my pistol. Now I intended to divert his attention and try to shoot him, but I was forestalled.

The crack of a gunshot rang from the undergrowth on our left and Sinclaire cursed and fell, tumbling past us down the steps.

'Quick, Watson!' shouted Holmes. 'Your pistol!'

Whipping out my Adams I snapped a shot at Sinclaire where he was scrambling to his feet at the bottom of the bank. My shot went wide, but he missed his own aim and darted backwards into cover.

Holmes and I slithered down the bank a few yards from the steps and surveyed the territory. Between us and the chalk-pits bent a siding, bearing a row of trucks loaded with chalk. The rails descended, joining the main line just beyond the foot crossing, and the space between the siding and the line was filled with tangled underbrush through which the footpath led. Our unknown ally had fired from somewhere along the siding. Sinclaire was now hidden somewhere in the brush.

Stealthily Holmes and I crept along the path, peering into the bushes on either side. We had gone only a few yards when a pistol cracked again and a bullet whistled past my head. Turning at the sound, I felt a second bullet tear at my left arm before I heard the shot. 'There, Holmes!' I shouted, for Sinclaire had somehow gained the advantage of the main line and was crouched low where the rails joined.

Holmes slid into the brush as the madman raised his gun again. I fired and missed, and another of his shots came uncomfortably close.

Flattening myself as far as I could, I sprawled and clambered up the embankment, hampered by my injured arm. As I reached the top and tried to gain my feet, I saw Sinclaire only yards away, his pistol bearing straight on me. I raised my own weapon, but there was no time.

Before he could fire, something astonishing occurred. The rails at his feet moved, throwing him off balance and leaving him sprawled headlong on the ballast of the track.

I climbed cautiously to my feet and walked towards him. His pistol lay some distance from his outstretched hand and he scrabbled for it madly. I could not see why he did not crawl towards it until I realised that his right foot was firmly trapped between the rail and the movable section of line that formed the junction with the siding.

I was still twenty feet from him when he reached his weapon. I fired quickly, but missed again. His first shot went wide, but the second caught me in the left shoulder, spinning me so hard that I lost my grip on my own pistol. I fell to my knees, fatigue and pain clawing at me. My head swam and I heard again the rhythmic clack of wheels as though I were back on the footplate at Salisbury. I knew that I must find my pistol, and turned in a daze to seek it. The sun flared in my eyes and I heard Holmes shout, 'Jump for your life, Watson!'

A second later Holmes sprang, seemingly out of the sun-dazzle, and grappled me in a rugby tackle that flung us both sideways on to the slope of the bank. Above me a rumbling filled the air and dark shapes whirled past along the siding, rattling down on the junction where Sinclaire lay trapped.

When he saw his fate he shrieked aloud, more horribly than I have ever heard a living creature scream, but his cry turned to a ghastly, throttled gurgle and was suddenly silenced as the train of heavy chalk-wagons ran remorselessly across the junction, smashing and tearing the hapless wretch to bloody tatters beneath their relentless iron wheels.

'Oh, dear God!' said the shocked voice of Emily Norton. 'I never intended that!'

THE WIND OF WAR

I lost my senses for a while, and the next I recall is Emily's anxious face above me as she dressed my wounds. Somehow she and Holmes had brought me across the railway line, and I lay on a couch in what must have been Sinclaire's study. When Emily saw that I had come to she summoned Holmes to my side.

'How are you, Watson?' he asked. 'Miss Norton says that both injuries are clean flesh wounds.'

With Emily's help I managed to sit up. 'I shall be all right, Holmes,' I assured him, 'but what of Sinclaire? What happened to him?'

'He is gone, Watson. King Edward's wish was carried out, not by us but by a blow of fate. The dead of Salisbury and Grantham and Shrewsbury are avenged in some small measure, and our country will not suffer from his murderous efforts in the coming struggle.'

My friend soon left to contact Mycroft, while Emily explored the Manor's kitchens in search of refreshment. I lay, nursing my injured shoulder, in the very lair of the astronomer and gazed about me. The quiet, comfortable room spoke of an educated country gentleman. Here were more display cases of fossils from the downs, fragments of meteorite, shelves and shelves of books on astronomy, geology and other sciences. By the window, its gleaming brass barrel pointed at the blue sky, stood his telescope on its ungainly folding legs. I could not fathom how madness such as Sinclaire's was nurtured in this scholarly nest, or how a man whose chosen studies were the wonders of the universe could descend to the horrors which he had engineered.

Emily brought tea and soon Holmes returned and began a search of Sinclaire's papers, occasionally crowing with delight as he unearthed some particularly significant document.

A party of Mycroft's functionaries arrived by motor car and I insisted on accompanying them to the railway siding.

Once there I could see how Sinclaire had died. The moving points had trapped his foot as he was about to fire on me, and his fall had caused a spiral fracture of the trapped leg. Whoever threw the lever that shifted the points had failed to realise that their action would release the train of loaded trucks, allowing them to run down the inclined siding on to the main line. Sprawled along the rail, Sinclaire with his injured leg could not even roll from their path. His remains were not a pretty sight.

Mycroft's men took charge and we left them to it. Strapping Emily's bicycle to our gig we set out for Newbury. My last glimpse of the Manor showed me the old bulldog, still asleep on the lawn as the afternoon shadows crept around it.

At Sandleford Water we solicited tea at the old inn on the Hampshire bank. It was served in a little garden, beside a tiny tributary of the Enborne and beneath gnarled apple trees already handsomely burdened. Beside the garden stood the hamlet's church and around the nearby green cottagers sunned themselves in their doorways. We sat around the rustic tea-table like three friends on a country excursion, and but for the pain in my shoulder I should not have believed the day's events.

'Now, gentlemen,' said Emily, once she had poured the tea, 'will somebody please explain what has been going on?'

Holmes smiled across his teacup at her. 'I believe', he said, 'that the fairer sex takes precedence. Perhaps you would like to enlighten us as to your sudden and very welcome appearance at Siddenton?'

'I wish I could mystify you as you enjoy mystifying others,' she said, 'but it was absurdly simple. The news was so worrying I wanted to know if you were making progress. I called at Claridge's this morning and was just pulling up there when you two lit out and grabbed a cab for Paddington.'

'You followed us!' I exclaimed. 'That was very daring!'

'Nonsense, doctor! I just knew that if you were in that kind of rush you must be on to something, so I followed without really

178

thinking. At Paddington I jumped into your train and followed you on to Newbury.'

'But how did you trace us from Newbury?' Holmes asked.

'I remembered that Siddenton Manor was on your list, so while you were at the livery stable I hired a bicycle and went on. You passed me by the station at Siddenton.'

'So we did!' I recalled.

'When you turned into the drive I parked my bicycle and went snooping. I saw the quarries and the siding and I thought someone there must know about blasting and about railways. I was walking up behind the wagons when I heard voices. I saw you on the crossing but I couldn't hear what was going on. I didn't see his gun until you moved. Then I guessed it was time to intervene.'

'You guessed rightly!' said Holmes.

'When he went down the steps, after my shot, I sneaked along behind the wagons, trying to see where he was, but I didn't see him till he stood up on the line. By then the doctor was in the way and I couldn't get a shot. I yanked the lever over because I saw he was right by the points and thought it would distract him and give Dr Watson a chance, it was pure luck it trapped his foot. I couldn't believe it!'

'Nor could I!' I remarked feelingly.

'Then I ran down behind the wagons. I saw him shoot you the second time, doctor, and then I realised the wagons were rolling away towards you both and I didn't know how it happened and I didn't know what to do!'

'At which point,' said Holmes, 'I had removed the chock from the first wagon, allowing them to move.'

Emily stared at him. 'You mean I didn't set them moving? I didn't kill him?'

'No, Miss Norton,' said Holmes. 'The loaded wagons were held at the top of the slope by a chock under the front wheels. Once it was removed they would inevitably run down. It is a common method of moving wagons without an engine. I set them moving, intending to provide a distraction, but I had not realised that Sinclaire was unable to move. So he met his end by a combination of chances, but he would have died in any case, and your prompt actions saved the far more valuable life of Dr Watson.'

179

Emily's eyes glowed as she smiled at both of us. 'Oh, I'm so glad it wasn't me! I thought I had done it and I couldn't bear to think of anyone – even him – dying like that.'

'He was insanely dangerous,' said Holmes, 'and his devilry had to be thwarted by whatever means.'

'How could a man of his attainments become a ruthless assassin?' I asked.

Holmes chuckled. 'You ask with Virgil – *Tantaene animis caelestibus irae*? Can there be such violence in celestial minds? Who knows what were the springs of his madness? The new doctors of the mind would say he blamed his father for his mother's death, but I doubt they could explain why a boy's love for his mother should become a murderous insanity. Still, he was evidently attached to his dead mother's country and prepared to destroy the symbols of his father's work. You recall that von Bork said Sinclaire never received payment?'

'But how did he become an agent of the Kaiser?' asked Emily.

'His papers contain correspondence with a professor of astronomy at Antwerp University, and he visited there frequently. Germany has one of her great spy schools in that city and that is probably where he was recruited and trained. No doubt they honed his knowledge of explosives, enabling him to supply the exceptionally clever devices used at Barrow and Portland.'

'You have not told us how you identified him in the end,' said Emily.

'Through a chance remark of Watson's,' said Holmes. 'I was reminded of a piece of data that I had ignored at the time and very nearly forgotten since. At the beginning of this affair I was convinced that a criminal explanation was unlikely. Misled by that premature assumption, I paid little attention to our landlady at Temple Combe when she prattled about her astronomer guest. When I knew the wrecks were deliberate, I recalled sufficient of her remarks to set me on the astronomer's trail, but overlooked the most significant comment.'

'What can that have been?' I asked.

'Our garrulous hostess, who admired your writings so much, Watson, told us that her husband read magazines passed on to him by the vicar, and in one of those he had read of the astronomer being "famous for something else". When you reminded me of Temple Combe it was a simple matter to find out the reading habits of the incumbent of Temple Combe, after which a minor outrage in the reading room at Claridge's put me in possession of these.'

He drew from his pocket two crumpled pages and spread them on the table.

'There is an interview with Edmund Sinclaire, then a prominent barrister who, having triumphed in his defence of Ansley Broughton in the Channel Islands Bank Fraud case, astounded the world by announcing his retirement to pursue an interest in the stars. There is his portrait and an account of his life and public career. They have been lying about in libraries for years, all unknown to me because I broke my own rule and theorised in advance of my data. It is a great lesson to me. This has not, I fear, been a successful case.'

'But you defeated him in the end,' said Emily.

A newspaper boy pedalled across the bridge from Newbury and I obtained an evening edition. Six German infantry brigades and two cavalry divisions had crossed the Belgian frontier. Britain had reminded Germany that we were both guarantors of Belgium's neutrality, demanding a reply by midnight. In Germany this was already seen as a declaration of war and a mob had attacked the British Embassy.

The grim news darkened the bright day. Across from us on the green, a cottager read pieces from the paper to his worried neighbours, and they called their children to them from their play, as though the threat were immediate. We paid our reckoning and set out for London.

At Paddington, only our *laissez-passers* obtained us a cab. The station was thronged with fearful holiday-makers returning from the west and reservists bound to join the colours. Already that presence of khaki, which now seems an inevitable part of life, was making itself apparent.

In the city the crowds had swelled again since morning, filling every street around Westminster. In the gathering dusk the lamplight gleamed with that peculiar luminescence that summer air imparts, gilding the leaves of trees and reflecting from ancient stonework, but it lit also the pale, worried faces of the people on the pavements.

Mycroft's department was ablaze with lights on every floor, as was every Government office in the area. Holmes' elder brother sat at his desk, dismissing two assistants as we were shown in. It was little more than a day since I had seen him last, but there were now dark shadows under his eyes and his features, always sharper than his plump form suggested, seemed even keener.

'Miss Norton, Sherlock, doctor,' he said, 'on this gloomy day it has been some relief to hear your news. You must tell me all about it. I seem to have been at this desk for days, and I feel sure that the office can arrange the war without me for a short while.'

He sent for tea, and while we took it Holmes outlined the last stages of his deductions and their outcome. Mycroft shook his head slowly at Holmes' description of the astronomer's death.

'So, it is finished,' he said, 'and we shall not have to contend with his efforts while we are at war. I do not know how to thank the three of you. You have all done this nation a great service, but one which I fear can never be publicly recognised.'

Emily and I murmured our protestations, while Holmes declared, 'It was no less than my duty, brother. I am sorry that my blindness at the beginning has drawn the thing out and cost lives that might have been spared.'

'You berate yourself unfairly,' replied Mycroft. 'The fault was mine – I was always of the opinion that the Plymouth train was deliberately wrecked, but I sought to mislead you. Then King Edward held back your hand, albeit for the best of reasons which today's events have proved genuine. The fact remains, Sherlock, that you prevented Sinclaire and his masters from destroying King Edward's plans – in that alone you delayed the war and helped us to be readier, stronger and with more allies. You have neutralised von Bork's operation and all of his agents will be arrested shortly. Finally, you put an end to Sinclaire's mad treachery. No, Sherlock – you must not regard this as a failure. I dare say that whatever deeds of devotion are done beneath our flag in the days ahead, none will deserve better of his country than you.'

I have rarely seen Holmes at a loss for words, but his brother's tribute left him so.

Emily broke the silence that followed. 'Is there now no hope?' she asked.

Mycroft looked up at the clock. 'Our ultimatum to the Kaiser expires at midnight in Berlin – eleven o'clock here. I imagine that in a very few minutes we shall be at war.'

We sat in silence, while the last few minutes of peace ticked away, until we heard Big Ben strike the fateful hour. Outside, the murmur of the crowd grew louder. Emily's dark eyes brightened with tears that ran unchecked down her cheeks.

'Oh! I am ashamed of my American blood tonight! We could so easily have stepped in and stopped this dreadful thing!'

'No one in any country has done more to stop it than you,' I told her. 'You may be ashamed of America, but if America could know she would be very proud of you!'

The crowd outside were singing the National Anthem. A tap at the door brought a clerk with a single sheet of paper. 'There has been no response from Berlin, sir,' he told Mycroft. 'This is the telegram that is going out.'

As he laid the copy on Mycroft's desk I could see its three short words:

WAR – ACTION – GERMANY

A few minutes later we left the weary Mycroft to his duties and Holmes and I escorted Emily to her hotel. With the passing of the deadline the flame of war had begun to work in the crowds. Their former stillness was gone; now they literally danced in the streets, singing songs from the old Queen's wars. Motor cars crammed with drunken youths and painted young women careered from bar to bar, their occupants shouting slogans and snatches of song. I wondered how these capering crowds would withstand the conflict that Mycroft foresaw.

Holmes prevailed on me to pass the night at Claridge's and I did not need much persuasion, for I was deeply tired and my wounded shoulder stung and ached.

So we finished that momentous day, sitting either side of a bottle of port, listening through the open window to the noise in the streets below.

'What will you do now, Watson?' asked Holmes, filling his pipe.

I touched my injured arm. 'When this has healed I shall see if my old service will have me. God knows, if your brother is right we shall need every doctor we can find. What of you, Holmes?'

'I shall go back to my bees and Martha and try to describe the art of detection before my memory fails me.'

We smoked in silence for a while, then Holmes rose and closed the window. 'There's an east wind coming, Watson,' he said.

'I think not, Holmes. It is very warm!'

'Good old Watson! You are the one fixed point in a changing age. There's an east wind coming all the same, such a wind as never blew upon England yet. It will be cold and bitter, Watson, and a good many of us will wither before its blast. But let us hope that it's God's own wind none the less, and a cleaner, better, stronger land will lie in the sunshine when the storm has cleared.'

So we came at last to the end of Holmes' final enquiry. We parted next morning, he to Sussex and I to Kensington, and I have not seen him since, though we have exchanged occasional notes. My wounds healed without complications and the Army Medical Service welcomed me back. Emily abandoned the stage and volunteered as a nurse, in which capacity I sometimes see her. She has no need now to be ashamed of her mother's country, since they have joined us in the struggle.

In this fourth year of war people are speaking of 'the war to end all wars' and I devoutly hope that it may be, and that, whenever this record is published, there may have been no repetition of the madness that now racks Europe. I cannot believe that men will not learn from the nightmare of Flanders, nor can I imagine that such a madman as the All Highest will ever again be permitted to drag a nation into such suicidal folly.

One thing is certain – history will remember the war. Let it also remember the part played in the struggle for peace by my friend Mr Sherlock Holmes.

EDITOR'S NOTES

I cannot, alas, state conclusively that this narrative is the work of Dr Watson, but I can offer readers a few of the fruits of my own researches into various aspects of the story which may help them to make up their own minds.

Chapter One
Most commentators accept that Holmes retired about the autumn of 1903, which does not disagree with the present account. However, there exists a record of a case, allegedly written by Holmes himself, called 'The Adventure of the Lion's Mane'. Published in 1926, it relates an incident in July of 1907 and contains the statement that 'At this period of my life the good Watson had passed almost entirely beyond my ken. An occasional weekend visit was the most I ever saw of him.' This does not, of course, entirely contradict the present narrative, but it does not confirm the account of 1907 given therein.

Some authorities question the authenticity of 'The Lion's Mane', because of an alleged scientific inaccuracy which makes its events extremely unlikely. It has been claimed that the Lion's Mane, a peculiarly beautiful and deadly jellyfish, would never have been found on the coast of Sussex, being a native of warmer waters. In fact, the opening of the Suez Canal gave the creature fresh pastures, and it is now found, not only on the south-eastern coast of Britain, but in the sea lochs of Scotland.

If that story is untrue, one must ask why it was written. Had it been written during the Great War, it might well have been created at Mycroft's behest (see Chapter Twenty-Three of the present narrative) to conceal Holmes' activities in 1907, but the date of publication argues against this. Was it, perhaps, written during the war but left unpublished until it found its way into the last group of Watson's records to appear, or did some question arise in the 1920s of Holmes' connection with the astronomer, leading to the publication of 'The Lion's Mane' to mislead someone?

Chapters Two and Three

The railway companies are those involved in the incidents at Salisbury and Grantham, but the directors who visited Holmes seem to be pseudonymous. Why is the fourth visitor never named? Was he someone of such notability that Watson felt unable to disguise him?

The descriptions of the two disasters agree with the details given in L.T. Rolt's study of British railway accidents, *Red For Danger* (Bodley Head, 1955; extended edition, Pan Books, 1982). By a curious coincidence, Rolt remarks that 'What precisely took place on the footplate of Ivatt Atlantic No. 276 on a September night those years ago is a question that Sherlock Holmes himself could not answer.'

Chapter Seven

Nowhere do we learn how the astronomer acquired the 'resinous opiate' with which he derailed three expresses. He was, however, a former criminal lawyer and a man of scientific hobbies with a library of scientific books. It is not impossible that he had acquired academic knowledge of obscure drugs, or that he had learned of some arcane opiate during his youth in South America. As recently as 1917 a specimen of the South American poison curare was exhibited in a criminal trial; the Crown Pathologist found no reliable modern literature on the drug and was forced to research accounts of seventeenth-century explorers.

Chapter Nine

If a special train did, indeed, take away two important passengers from the scene of the Grantham crash, it remains a secret. Nevertheless, King Edward VII did travel in a Mercedes and nurtured a passion for ginger biscuits (French ones, for preference, but one supposes they would have been unobtainable in Grantham by day, let alone in the middle of the night).

A minor mystery revolves around the curmudgeonly Grocer Roberts, who would not give the Great Northern a few pennorth of credit. He was certainly not one of my ancestors. One wonders whose ancestor he may have been.

Chapter Twelve

The Variety Artists' Federation has no record of Emily Norton, under that name or as Eileen Neagle. Perhaps some researcher into Edwardian music hall may be able to unearth the real name of this outstanding lady.

Watson never reveals (and apparently did not know) what happened to the German prisoner at Balmoral. It is difficult to imagine that he was executed in secret, with the King's connivance. Perhaps, like Howard Hugo, he passed the years till 1918 in that 'clinic' in Surrey.

Chapter Thirteen

A secret tunnel into the heart of Windsor Castle? Yes, there was such a tunnel, which certainly existed in the early years of this century. Its structure was as Watson describes and it emerged in the home of one of the royal chaplains within the walls. Royal sources said at the time that the far end (wherever it was) had been blocked, but they would say that, wouldn't they, and why did they keep it gas-lit if it couldn't be used? Whether it has survived the recent fire, I know not, but one account of the disaster said that fire-fighters were hampered by the fire sweeping through passages and tunnels within the walls.

While most of the political background of the story is a matter of record (King Edward's wooing of the French and the Russians is certainly true), the idea that there were negotiations between the King and anyone in the United States casts a new light on the period.

Who was Theobald G. Evans? The name is one of Watson's inventions, as is the 'Evans Arizona Trust Bank'. It is the case that, when British funds ran low during the war, American banks assisted, but there has been no other evidence of any prior agreement to do so. If Evans could be properly identified it might assist in tracing his great-niece (and, probably, her famous mother).

Chapter Fourteen
As far as I have been able to check, none of the suspects in Holmes' list existed under the names given and many of the place-names are false. Presumably Watson, with his customary discretion, was avoiding embarrassment to all of the innocent while concealing the real identity of the maniac.

Chapter Fifteen
The account of the Shrewsbury crash agrees with L.T. Rolt's version of the event.

A dramatic photograph of the Shrewsbury wreck, apparently taken early on the morning after, exists and can be seen (among other places) in John Westwood's *Pictorial History of Railways* (Bison Books, 1988). Some believe that it includes the only known photograph of Holmes and Watson, standing to the left of a group of gentlemen in the centre of the picture. If that is true it is particularly unlucky that both have their backs to the camera.

Chapter Eighteen
A puzzling feature of the narrative is the bombing of the Diogenes Club. Watson says that five members were killed, all of them, presumably, men of some status if they belonged to the Diogenes Club, yet I cannot find any record of the incident. Nor have I been able to trace the newspaper that ran a special edition on the outrage. Such an edition would not have been unusual (the *News of the World*, a Sunday paper, ran a teatime special to announce the capture of Crippen).

Chapter Nineteen
Alexander Snelwar, Steinie Morrison and Leon Beron were real, as was the Warsaw Restaurant. Watson evidently felt no need to disguise names that became well known during Morrison's trial.

The best evidence for the authenticity of the story is the identification of 'Peter the Painter' as Gederts Eliass. The theory that Eliass (who later became a prominent artist in the Soviet Union) was the Painter was first made public in 1988. By then the manuscript had been in my possession for a number of years and, if I am believed on this point, there can be little doubt that it is really Watson's work.

Whether Leon Beron was a spy for the Czar must remain a matter of speculation, as it has been for years.

Peter Hahn, the Deptford baker, was a German spy who stood trial in 1917 alongside a colleague called Muller. Muller was executed but Hahn, a British citizen born in Battersea, received seven years.

Chapter Twenty

The murder of Leon Beron is accurately described and none of Holmes' theories about it are impossible. See 'The Trial of Steinie Morrison' in the *Notable British Trials* series (William Hodge, 1922), Eric Linklater's *The Corpse on Clapham Common* (Macmillan, 1971), and *Stinie, Murder on the Common* by Andrew Rose (Bodley Head, 1985; Penguin, 1989).

Morrison certainly did work in bakeries, but there is no provable connection between him and Peter Hahn.

Another confirmation of the manuscript's authenticity comes from Athelney Jones' information. He can only have been referring to the investigation of a family called Wheeldon, who were brought to a secret trial in Derby in 1917, accused of conspiracy to assassinate Lloyd George. An agent of the Ministry of Munitions Counter-Espionage Division is said to have discovered the plot. He did not give evidence at the trial, where he was referred to as 'Alex Gordon'. However, the defendants claimed that 'Gordon' was none other than Steinie Morrison – on the face of it a preposterous claim, for Morrison was still, supposedly, in prison.

After the conviction of the Wheeldons, a radical newspaper began a campaign of vilification against 'Gordon', who came out of hiding and went to Derby to shoot the editor. He failed, but gave an interview to another paper, in which he said that he had acted against the Wheeldons because the Government had some powerful hold over him. The Government was so embarrassed that he was sent to South Africa, where he was murdered. The 'real' Morrison died in prison in 1921.

The connection between Morrison and the Wheeldons was first brought to light in a documentary play at Derby Playhouse in 1973, by which time the present manuscript had been in the possession of my family for many years.

Chapter Twenty-One

Whoever Emily's great-uncle was, his contacts were good. The men named in his cipher were the Kaiser's agents in the States who made contact with Irish-American nationalists.

If you share Watson's difficulty in working out the source of the code, it was the first chapter of *A Study in Scarlet* as it appeared in Beeton's Christmas Annual for 1887 – the chapter entitled 'Mr Sherlock Holmes'.

Chapter Twenty-Three

When the Fleet returned to Portland from summer manoeuvres, Churchill ordered them to Scapa Flow, so that they could command the North Sea if needed. They sailed as Watson describes them, in a convoy eighteen miles long. Churchill's action, unauthorised by the Cabinet, caused a split in the Liberal Government and provoked resignations.

Chapter Twenty-Four

Who was Maximilian von Bork? He does not appear in any list of German agents in Britain at that period, yet he was obviously the head of the network. Presumably Holmes' representations on the German's behalf permitted him to leave Britain discreetly. Perhaps a search of the membership records of East Anglian hunts would reveal a German member who was the master-spy.

The success of Holmes' pose as 'Altamont' is evidenced by the fact that virtually every German spy in Britain was known to British Intelligence by the outbreak of war.

Watson does not name the powerful official in whose office Holmes questioned von Bork, but his description gives the game away. It must have been Sir Basil Thompson's room at the Yard. Thompson later claimed that every real or suspected German spy caught in Britain had sat in his brown leather armchair.

Chapter Twenty-Five

The most infuriating chapter of all! Sinclaire is a false name, no Siddenton Manor existed in north Hampshire, but there were chalk-pits in the downs in that area.

The journey from Newbury can be followed to where the

present A34 passes between Beacon Hill and Watership Down. It seems that the turn-off was the lane that leads to Old Burghclere. There was a station there on the Didcot, Newbury and Southampton line (called, confusingly, Burghclere. The station for Burghclere, north of the downs, was called, even more confusingly, Highclere).

Near to Old Burghclere lies Sydmonton Court, the present home of the composer Sir Andrew Lloyd Webber, but it does not match the details given of "Siddenton Manor". Sydmonton Court has its own secret and sinister history. Men from an American labour battalion, billeted there in World War Two, robbed the armoury one night and ambushed a military police sergeant outside a village pub. He and a number of civilians were killed by gunfire. The entire episode was kept secret until recently, to avoid damaging Anglo-American relations.

The inn by Sandleford Water is definitely The Swan in the hamlet of Newtown. The ford and the graceful wooden bridge have been long replaced by a stone bridge which can be found on the A34 where it crosses from Berkshire into Hampshire.

I do not believe that I can assist the reader further, except to state that I am as satisfied as I can be that the narrative is a genuine and important work of John H. Watson and records a hitherto incompletely known case. Others may reach different conclusions.

Barrie Roberts, September 1993.